WEBTOON

LEARN TO DRAW

True Beauty.

Yaongyi

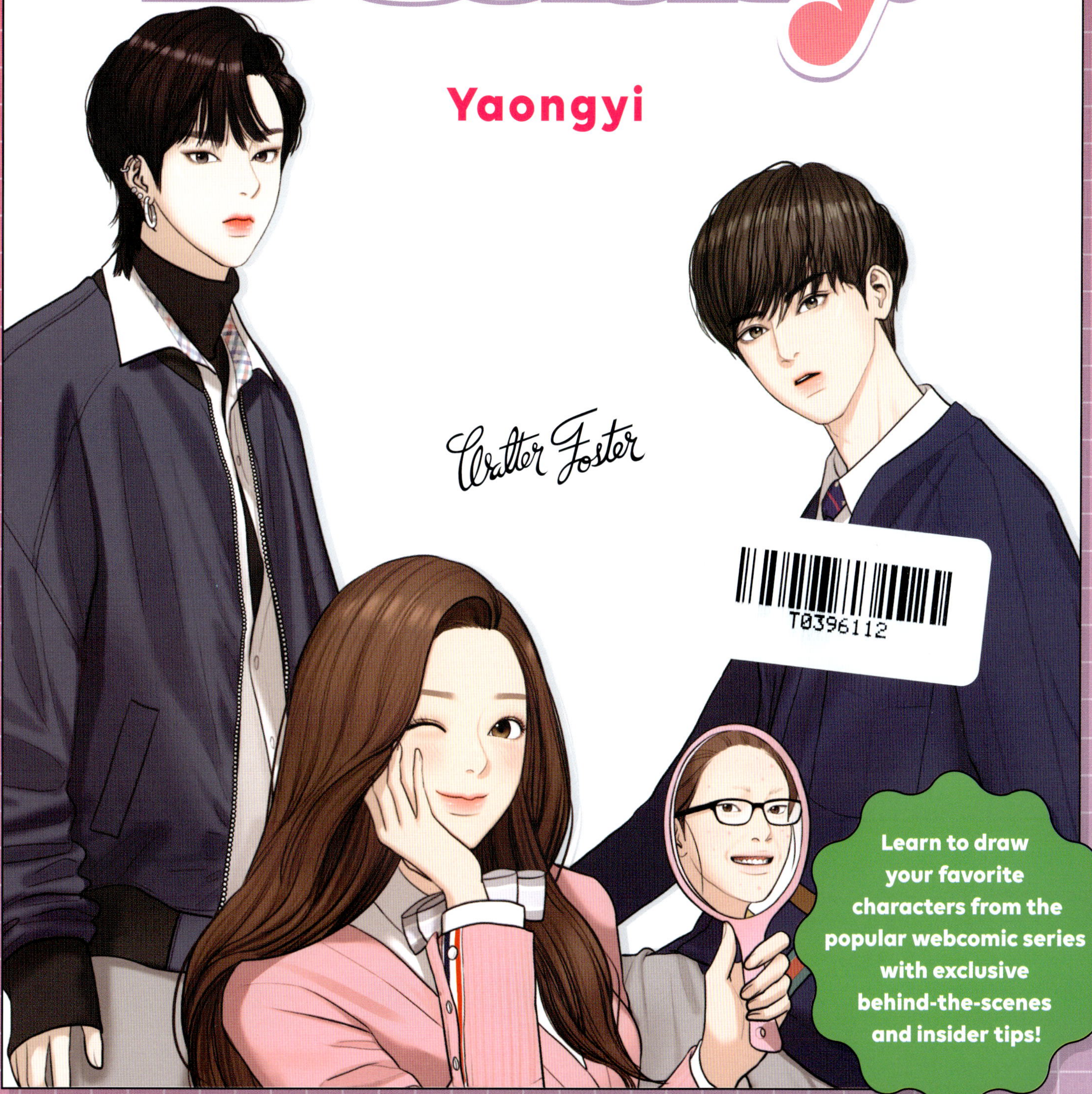

Walter Foster

Learn to draw your favorite characters from the popular webcomic series with exclusive behind-the-scenes and insider tips!

Quarto.com | WalterFoster.com

© 2024 Quarto Publishing Group USA Inc.
WEBTOON TRUE BEAUTY © Yaongyi. All rights reserved.
WEBTOON and all related trademarks are owned by WEBTOON Entertainment Inc. or its affiliates.

First Published in 2024 by Walter Foster Publishing, an imprint of The Quarto Group,
100 Cummings Center, Suite 265-D, Beverly, MA 01915, USA.
T (978) 282-9590 F (978) 283-2742

All rights reserved. No part of this book may be reproduced in any form without written permission of the copyright owners. All images in this book have been reproduced with the knowledge and prior consent of the artists concerned, and no responsibility is accepted by producer, publisher, or printer for any infringement of copyright or otherwise, arising from the contents of this publication. Every effort has been made to ensure that credits accurately comply with information supplied. We apologize for any inaccuracies that may have occurred and will resolve inaccurate or missing information in a subsequent reprinting of the book.

Walter Foster Publishing titles are also available at a discount for retail, wholesale, promotional, and bulk purchase. For details, contact the Special Sales Manager by email at specialsales@quarto.com or by mail at The Quarto Group, Attn: Special Sales Manager, 100 Cummings Center, Suite 265-D, Beverly, MA 01915, USA.

10 9 8 7 6 5 4 3 2 1

ISBN: 978-0-7603-8969-0

Digital edition published in 2024
eISBN: 978-0-7603-8970-6

Library of Congress Cataloging-in-Publication Data is available.

Step-by-step artwork: Ryan Axxel
WEBTOON Rights and Licensing Manager: Amanda Chen
Design, layout, and editorial: Christopher Bohn, Gabriel Thibodeau, and Coffee Cup Creative LLC
Copyediting: Susan H. Greer
Illustrations and art: Yaongyi and WEBTOON Entertainment, except Shutterstock on cover (background) and pages 24 and 25.

Printed in China

CONTENTS

DRAWING STEP BY STEP.....34

INTRODUCTION TO WEBCOMICS.....90

INTRODUCTION.....4

FROM THE CREATOR.....6

THE CHARACTERS.....8

GETTING STARTED.....22

ABOUT THE CREATOR.....96

INTRODUCTION
Immerse your self in the enchanting world of True Beauty.

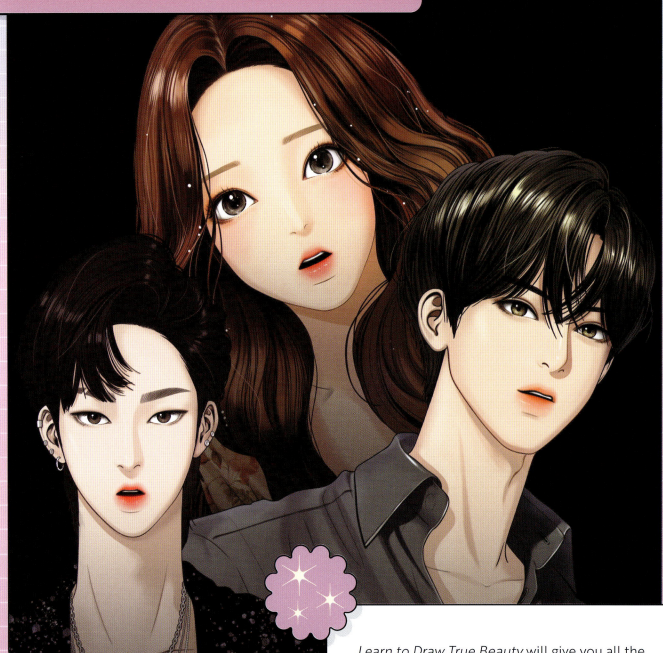

Learn to Draw True Beauty will give you all the feels. Welcome to a beautiful world of self-esteem, love, and learning to accept yourself for who you are.

What Is True Beauty?

After binge-watching beauty videos online, a shy comic-book fan masters the art of makeup and becomes her school's prettiest girl overnight, skyrocketing her social standing. But will her elite status be short lived? How long can she keep her real self a secret? And what about that cute boy who knows what she's hiding?

Check out the latest episode of the hit WEBTOON series.

SYNOPSIS

Jugyeong is an introverted high school student whose life takes an unexpected and astonishing turn when she uncovers the magic of online makeup tutorials. Follow along as she navigates the intricate labyrinth of high school life as well as a riveting love triangle. Who can resist both a mystery man and a bad boy?

Whether you're an aspiring illustrator or an ardent fan eager to capture the essence of *True Beauty* through your artwork, this guide is tailor-made to unlock your potential. Learn from the creator of this smash hit about learning to accept yourself as you are.

What Is a Webcomic?

Webcomics are comics published on a website or mobile app.

Meet WEBTOON™.

We started a whole new way to create stories and opened it up to anyone with a story to tell. We're home to thousands of creator-owned series with amazing, diverse visions from all over the world. Get in on the latest original romance, comedy, action, fantasy, horror, and more from big names and big-names-to-be—made just for WEBTOON. We're available anywhere, anytime, and always for free.

FROM THE CREATOR

What was your inspiration behind creating your WEBTOON series?

Honestly, I feel I have to acknowledge that I got lucky. I was looking for a project and a new business venture—something creative and fulfilling—and that's where it all started. I'm delighted the series has grown to reach so many readers!

What inspired you to create True Beauty?

When I first started, I reviewed seasonal fashion shows of various luxury brands and made predictions about future makeup trends. I'd pour over fashion spreads and articles for inspiration.

Is there advice you would give your fans when trying to draw your characters or starting their own series?

Don't be afraid to try! I believe one of the best things you can do is simply draw. Make your art and submit it wherever you can. Getting started is the first half of the journey, and what's more exciting than creating webcomics?!

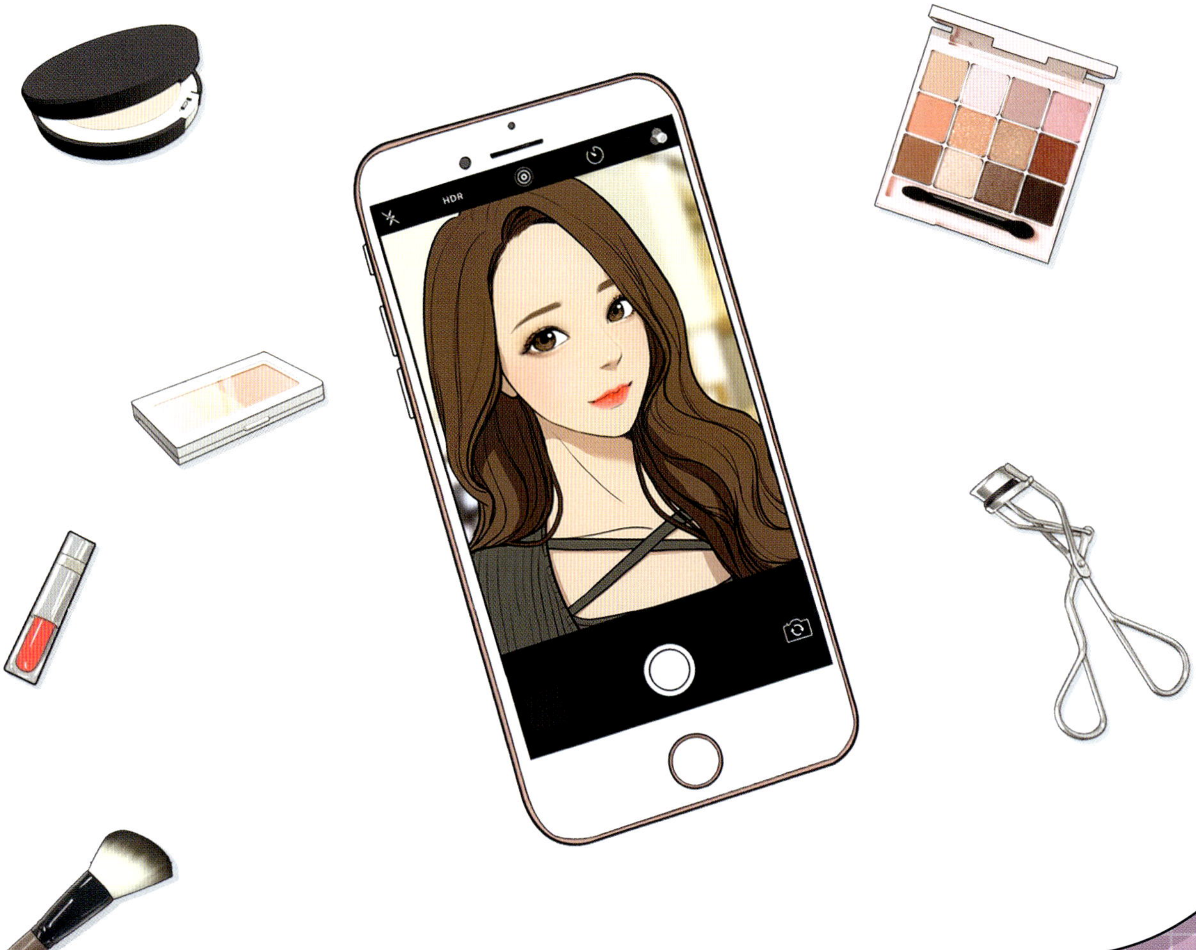
HDR

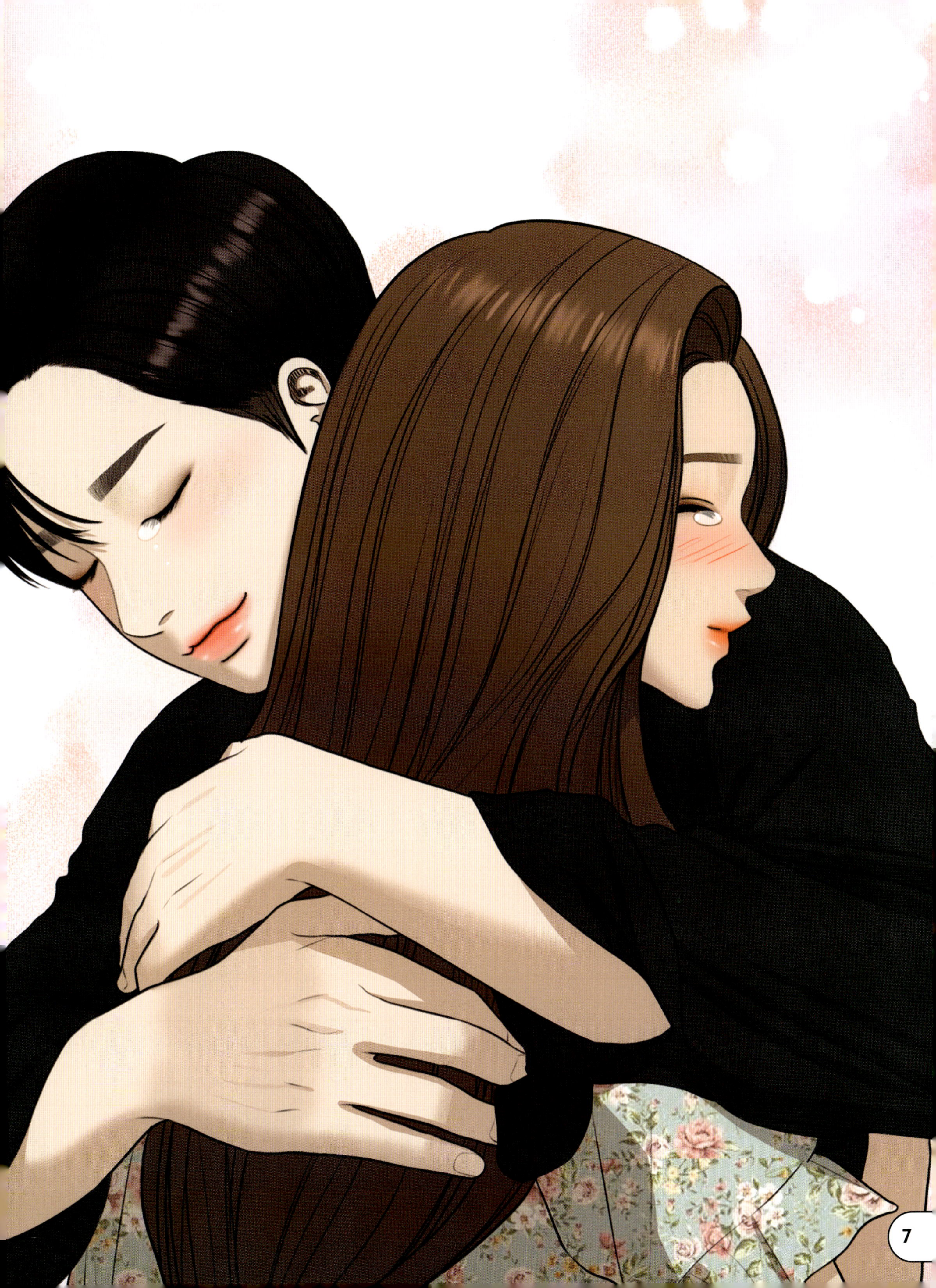

THE CHARACTERS

Meet the cast of True Beauty.

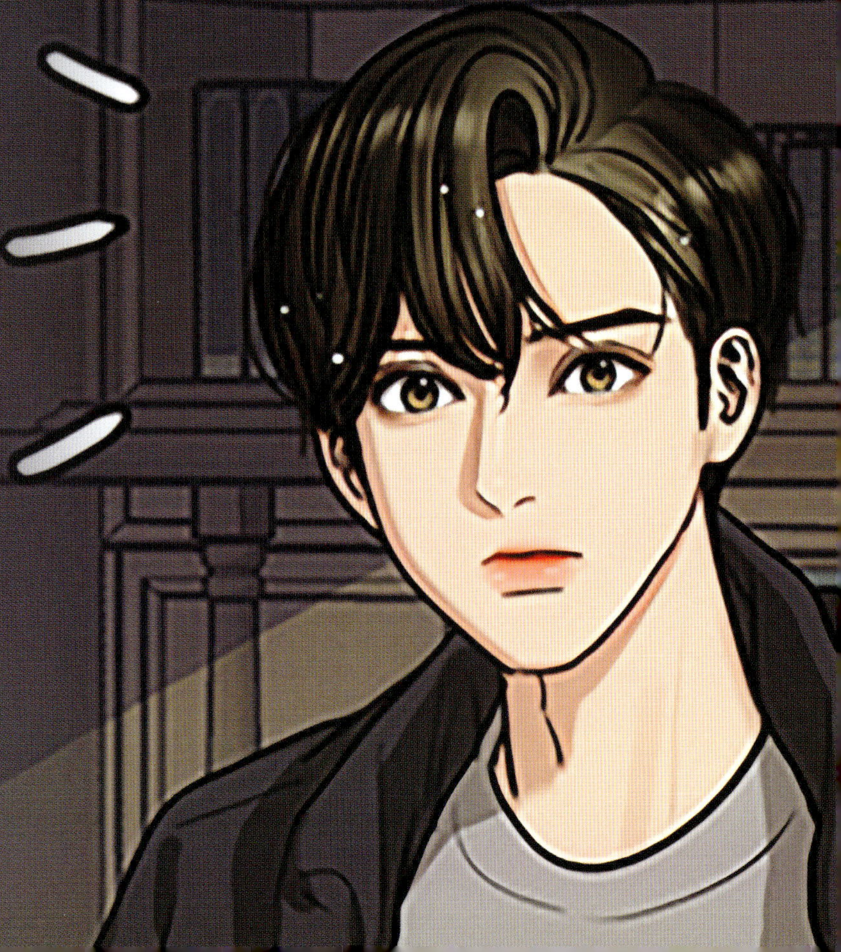

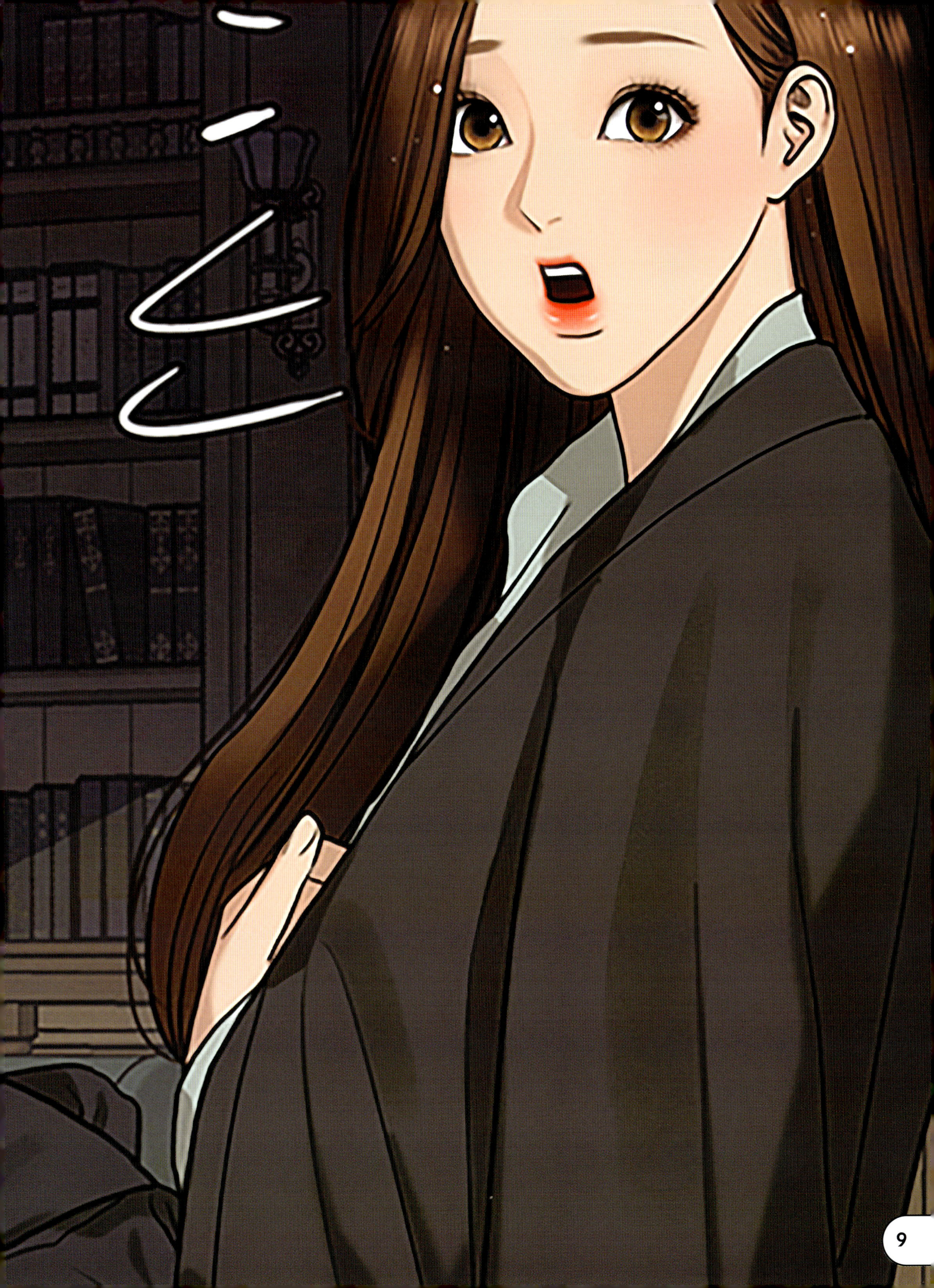

Jugyeong

Natural

Background

Jugyeong's glamorous transformation has changed her life! But with the change comes a ton of stress. From a notoriously good-looking family, Jugyeong is constantly self-conscious about her appearance, and she remains distraught that others might see her bare face. When she rises to fame as the most beautiful girl at Saebom High School, she concocts a plan to keep her true face hidden from the whole school. She never leaves the house without makeup unless she is alone or just with her family.

Appearance

When she's not wearing makeup, Jugyeong usually ties her hair into a ponytail and wears loose-fitting clothes like sweatpants. Like many people, Jugyeong has oily skin prone to acne—hence the BB cream—and she shaves her eyebrows almost completely, leaving only two very thin lines to be filled in with a brow pencil.

COLOR PALETTE

HAIR HIGHLIGHT	HAIR MIDTONE	HAIR UNDERTONE	SKIN
#9B644E	#6A4838	#33211A	#EFC7AD

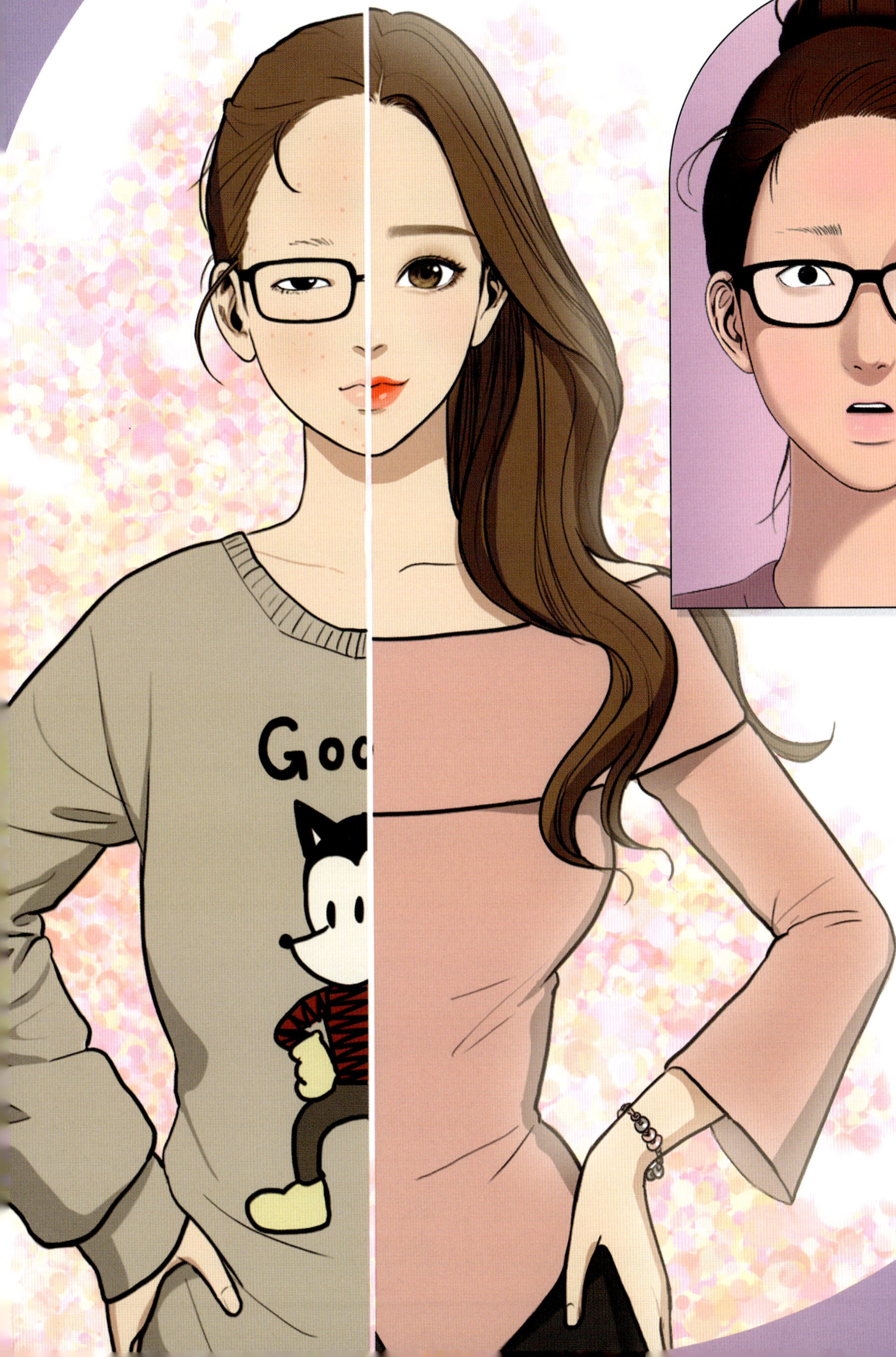
Goo

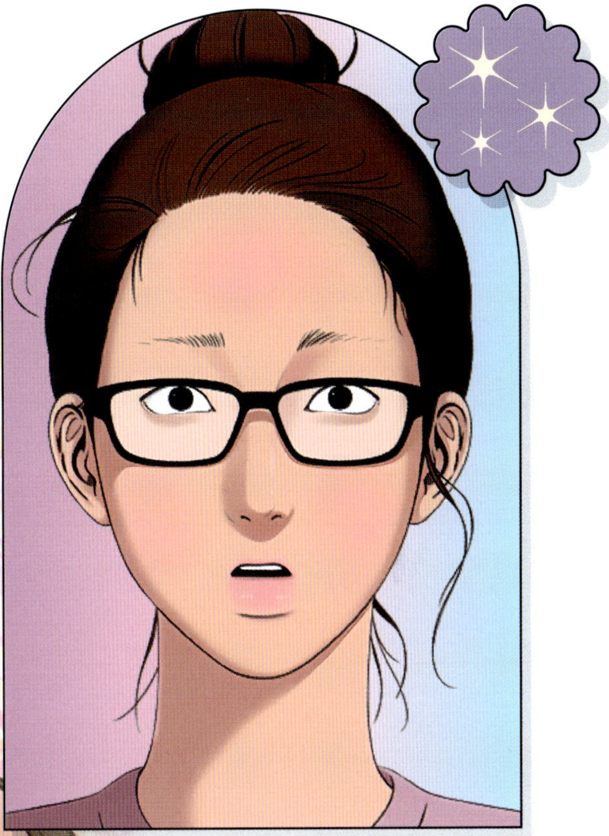

Jugyeong
Makeup

Appearance

With makeup, Jugyeong is considered the most beautiful girl around. She has large light brown eyes, long hair, and straight eyebrows.

When applying makeup to create her gorgeous look, she uses BB cream, a brown eyebrow pencil, brown eyeshadow, brown eyeliner, peach-colored blush, and a glossy coral lip tint. She uses an eyelash curler, mascara, and even glue to apply false eyelashes. She also wears brown-tinted contact lenses instead of glasses. Unless it's a special occasion, Jugyeong keeps her makeup so natural that others believe she isn't wearing any at all.

When it comes to fashion, Jugyeong is careful to match the overall tone of her makeup and outfits so they coordinate and complement each other.

COLOR PALETTE

HAIR HIGHLIGHT	HAIR MIDTONE	HAIR UNDERTONE	SKIN
#9B644E	#6A4838	#33211A	#EFC7AD

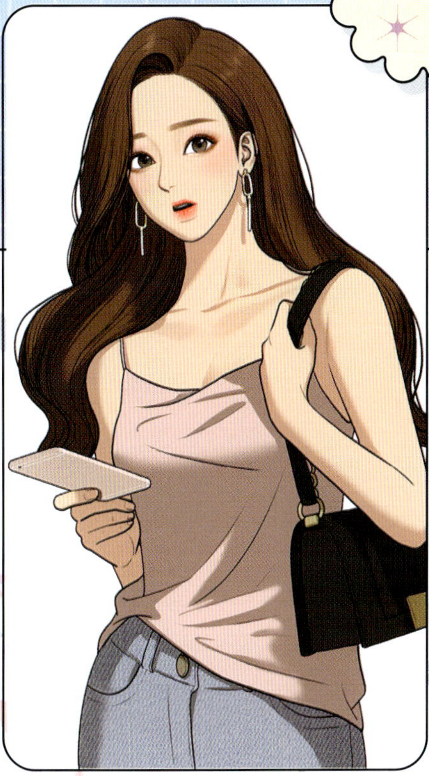

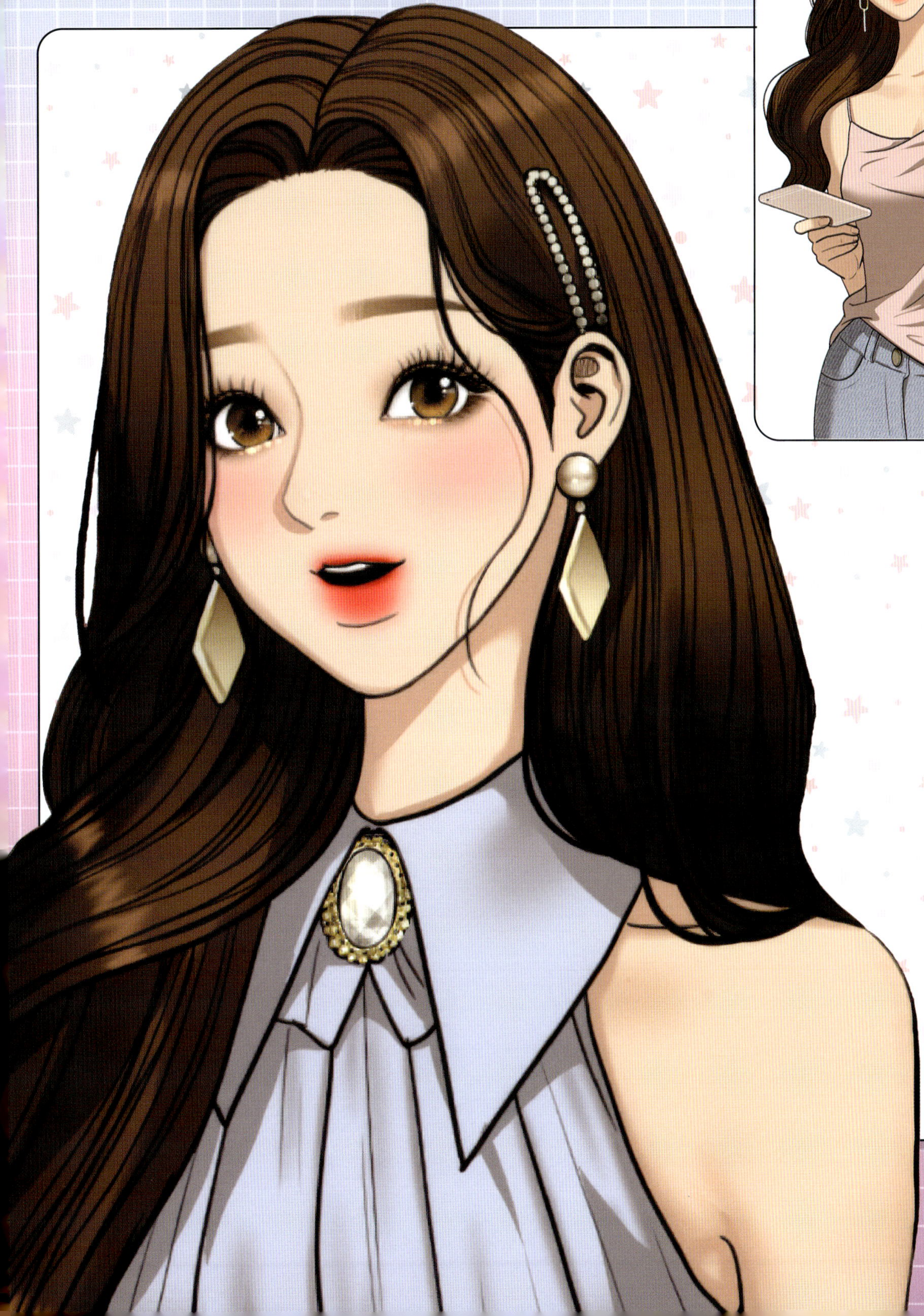

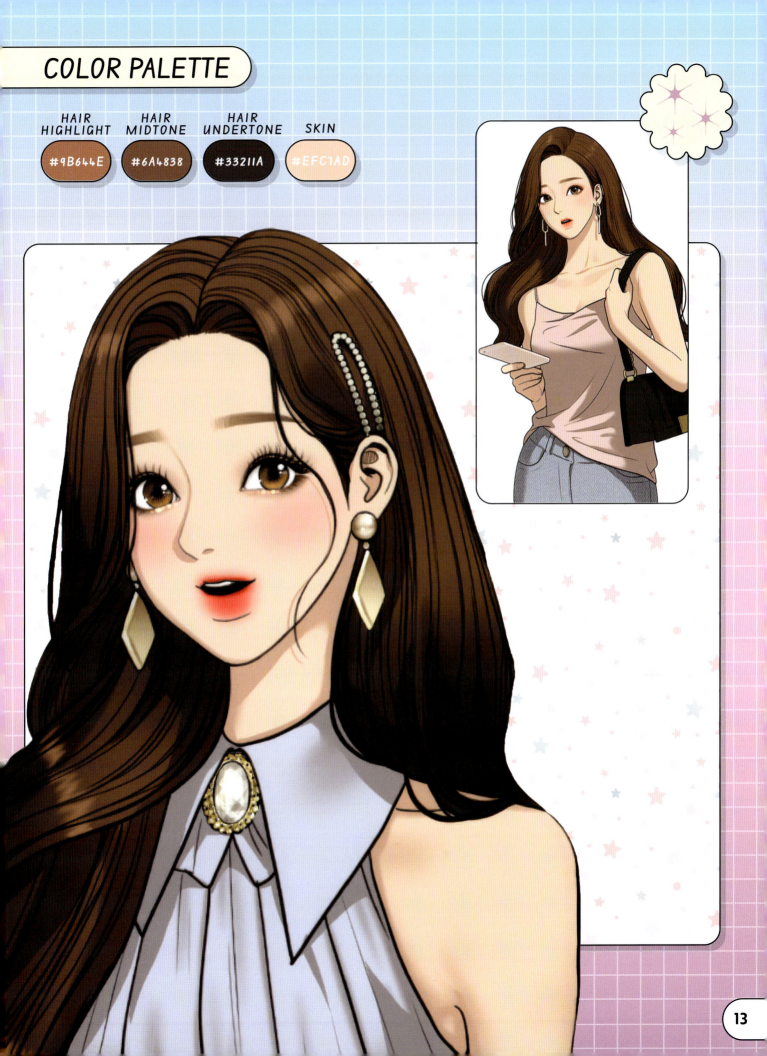

Suho

Background

Suho is the son of Lee Joo-heon, a famous Korean actor, and a Japanese woman named Yuko. After his family moves to South Korea from Japan, Suho transfers to a South Korean middle school, where he's constantly bullied by his classmates for his heritage. Seo-jun saves him from the torment, sparking a close friendship between the two of them.

Suho finds it difficult to shake his impulses—only speaking when necessary and rarely considering other people's feelings. However, after meeting and developing a crush on Jugyeong, Suho reveals a softer, more loving side.

Appearance

Suho is tall and exotic, with dark brown hair and light hazel eyes. He is the definition of the classic handsome type. He has thick, masculine lines, yet a delicate and pretty face. Many people consider him handsome, but Suho doesn't seem to care. He instead busies himself with fashionable clothes from luxury brands—mostly shirts paired with jeans or slacks. He tends to keep his outfits low-key, as his features are rather eye-catching.

COLOR PALETTE

HAIR HIGHLIGHT	HAIR MIDTONE	HAIR UNDERTONE	SKIN
#8A7A5F	#454035	#252420	#EFC7AD

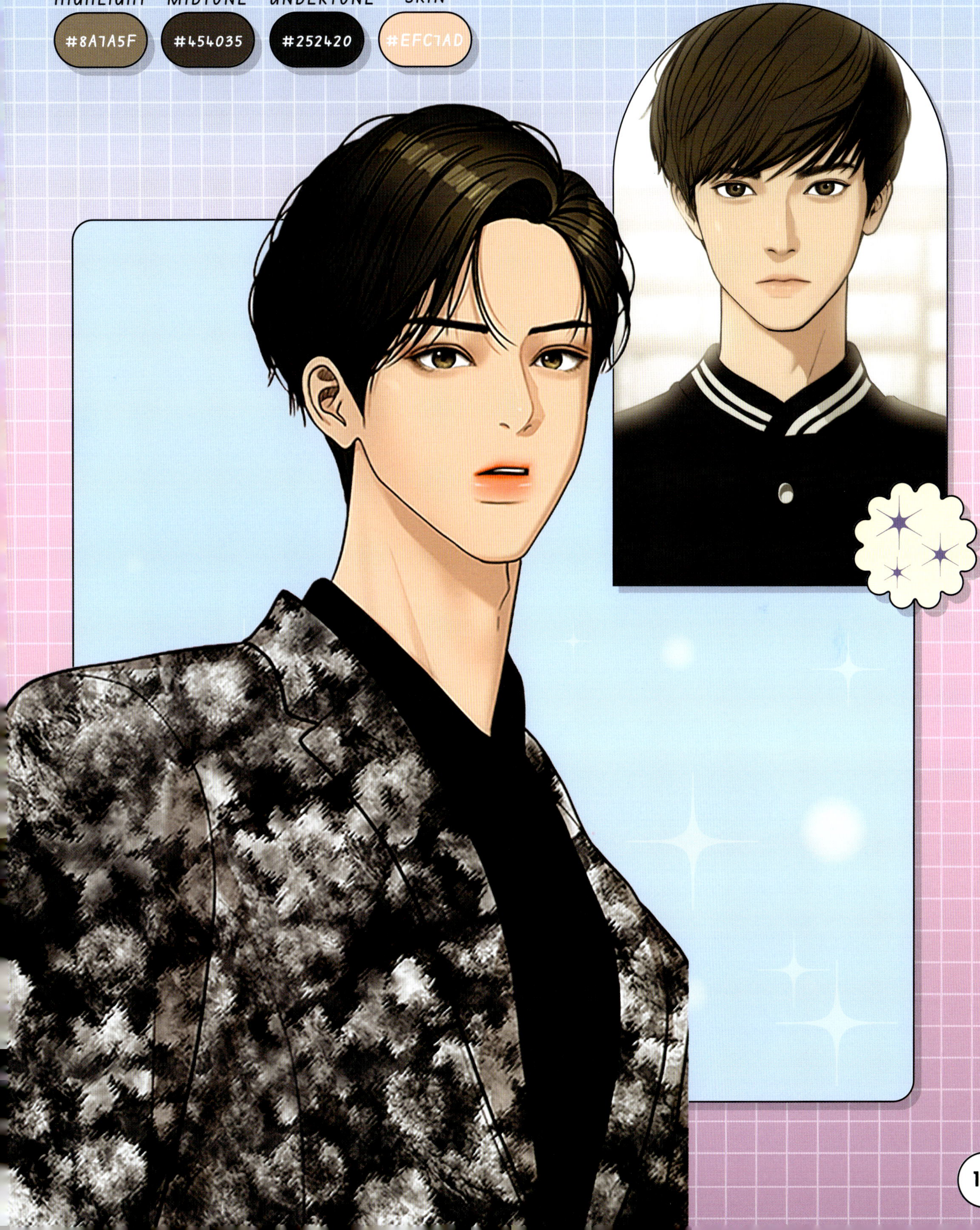

Seo-jun

Background

Meet Seo-jun, Jugyeong's boyfriend. In middle school, he's best friends with Suho but, due to a series of contentious events, their friendship falls apart. When Suho moves to Japan, Seo-jun fails to reach out, causing the two to lose touch.

Seo-jun is a cold and sometimes rude person, but he is very warm and friendly to his friends and family. When showing affection, he tends to have a *tsundere* attitude, hiding his true feelings with jokes and teasing. He acts tough in front of others but is sensitive and easily embarrassed. Having grown up in a low-income family, Seo-jun's greatest concern and goal is to achieve financial stability. Luckily for him, he is an idol trainee at ST Entertainment, an endeavor Suho supports before their falling out.

Appearance

Seo-jun is tall with broad shoulders and long legs. His hair is black with bangs that sweep across his forehead. Quite handsome, he has a fashion model vibe and a style that stands out in a crowd. To contrast with his fair skin, he often wears black clothing. His aloof demeanor paired with his good looks often cause people to mistake him for a superstar.

COLOR PALETTE

HAIR HIGHLIGHT	HAIR MIDTONE	HAIR UNDERTONE	SKIN
#635050	#271A1E	#000000	#F3D4C2

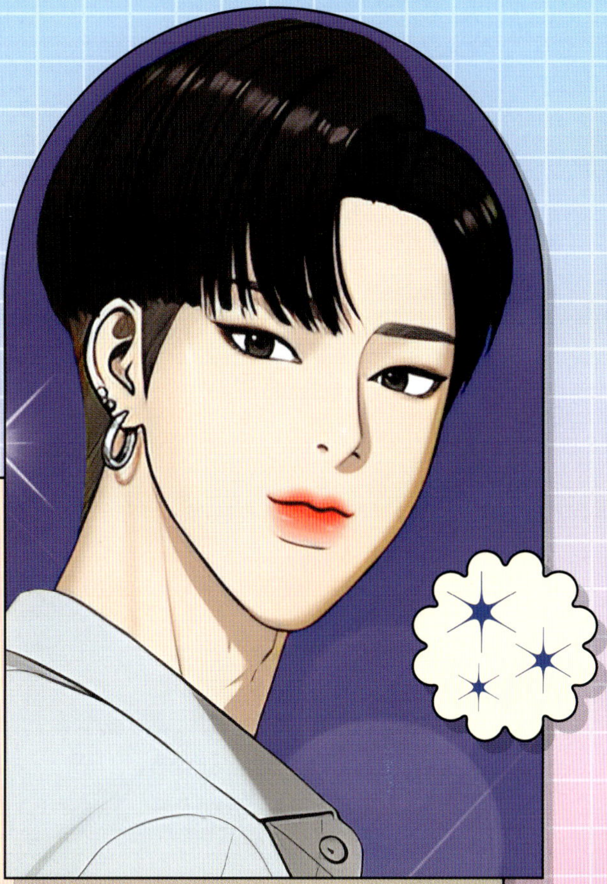

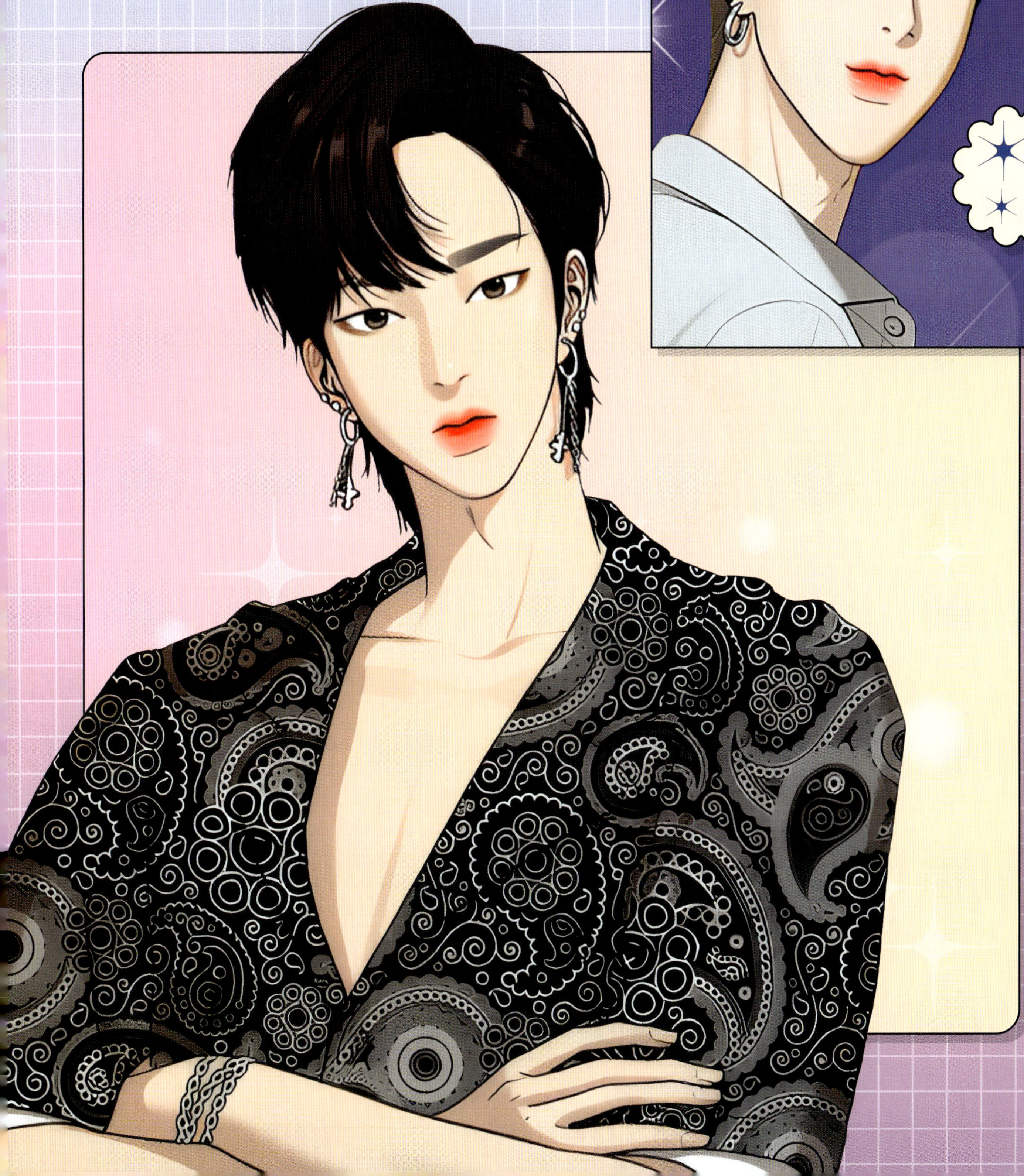

The Trio

As in most stories worth reading, the relationships between Jugyeong, Suho, and Seo-jun are dynamic and complicated. Each character is at odds with their own identity in different ways. Jugyeong struggles to grasp the meaning of true beauty, Suho works to fully embrace his cultural heritage, and Suho reconciles his complicated relationship to money and fame. These three young creatives find themselves smack in the middle of a star-crossed coming-of-age story more real and truly beautiful than they might even understand.

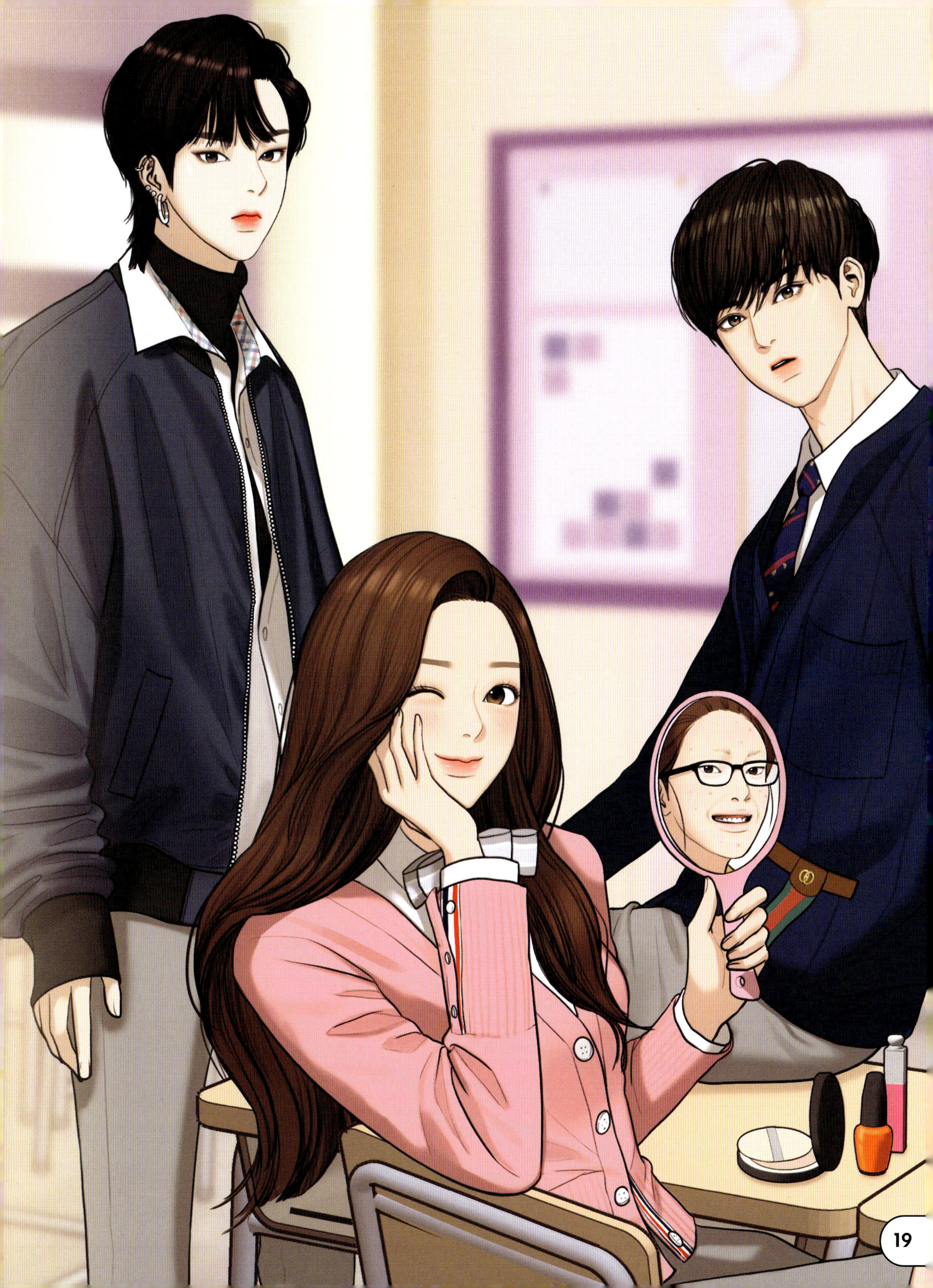

Character Height Chart

When developing a cast of characters for a story, it is good to map out how tall they are in relation to each other so you can keep consistency when drawing them together in various scenes.

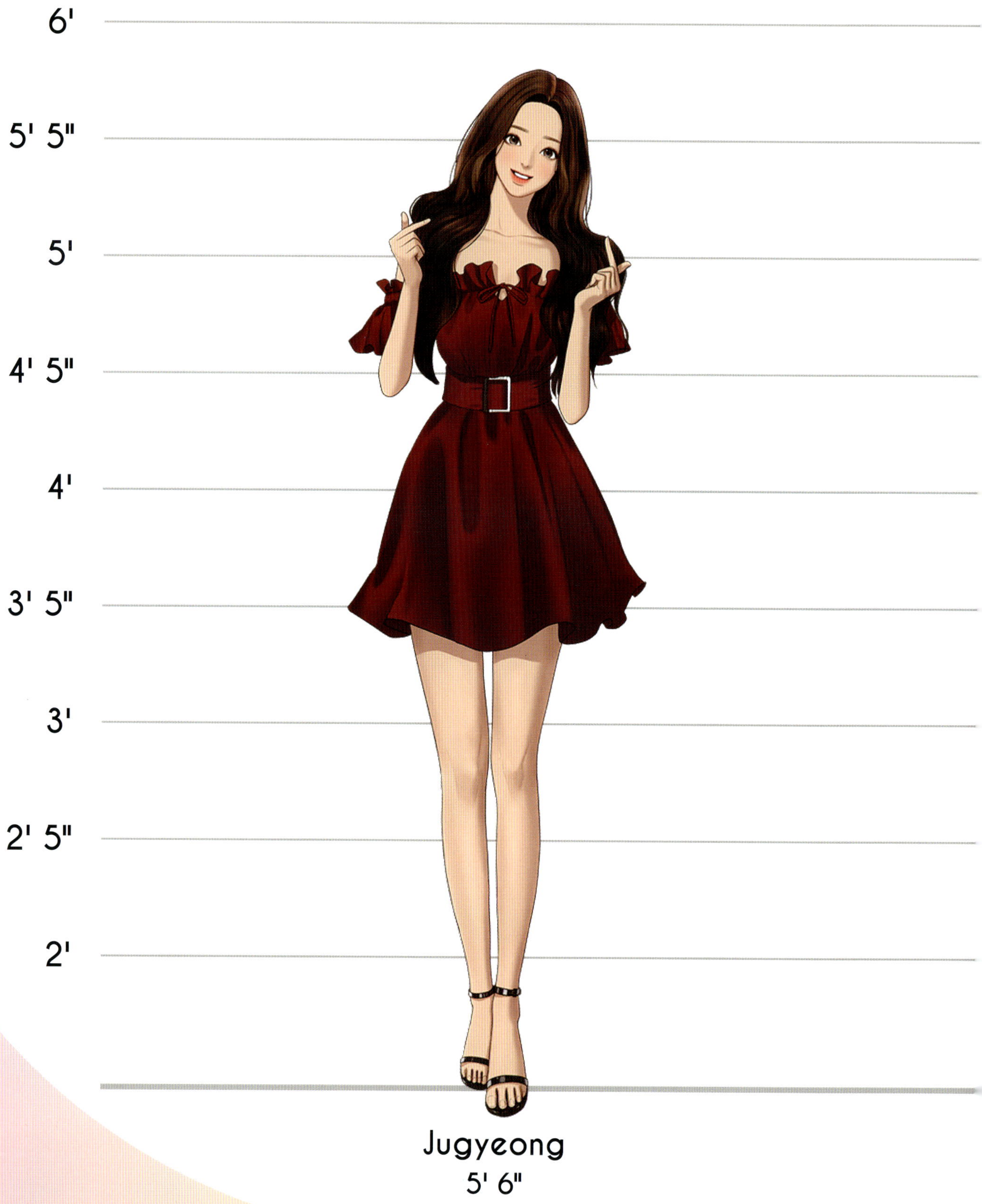
6'
5' 5"
5'
4' 5"
4'
3' 5"
3'
2' 5"
2'
Jugyeong
5' 6"

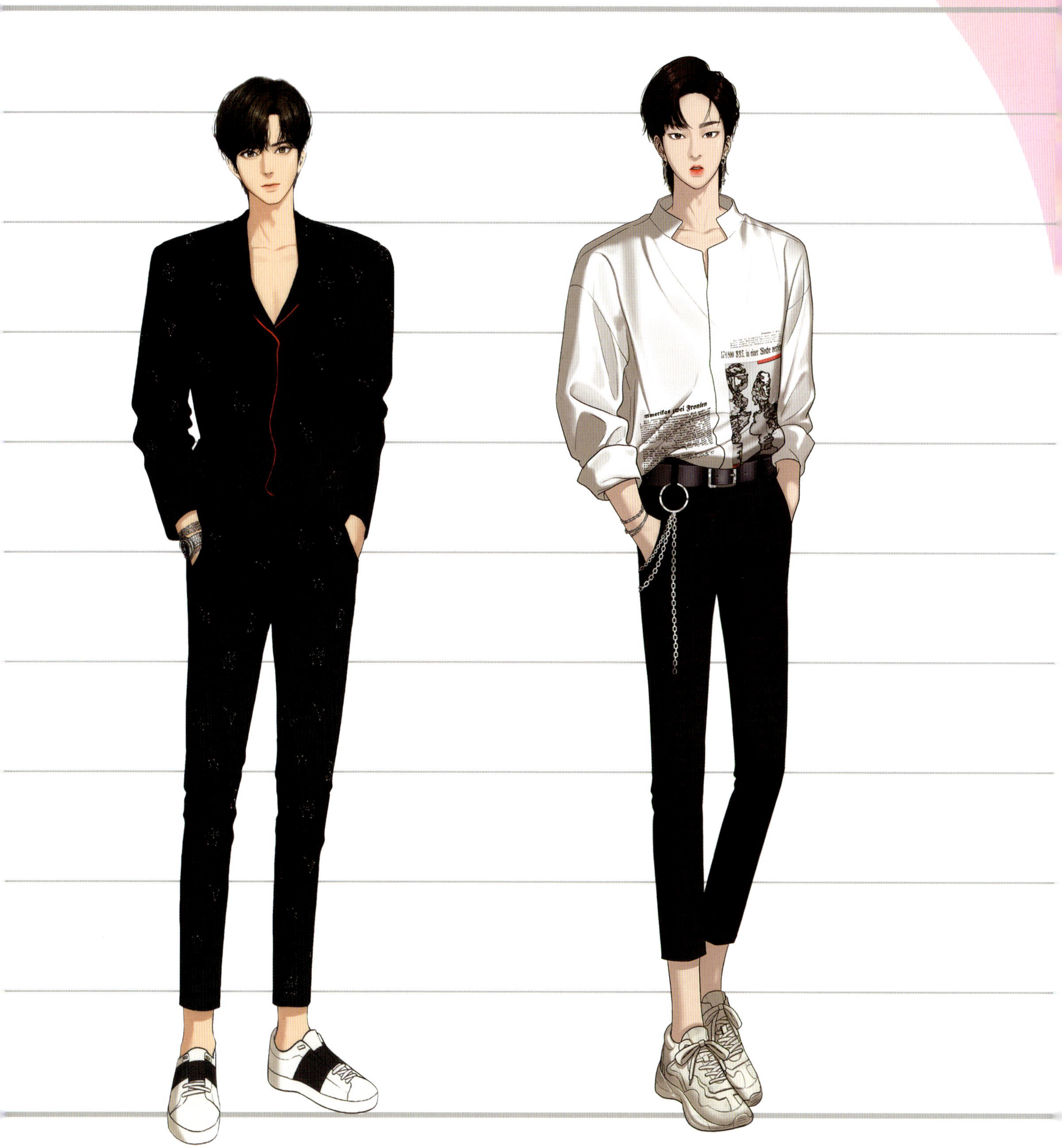

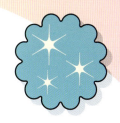

Suho
6' 2"

Seo-jun
6' 3"

GETTING STARTED

Learn about the coloring and drawing process.

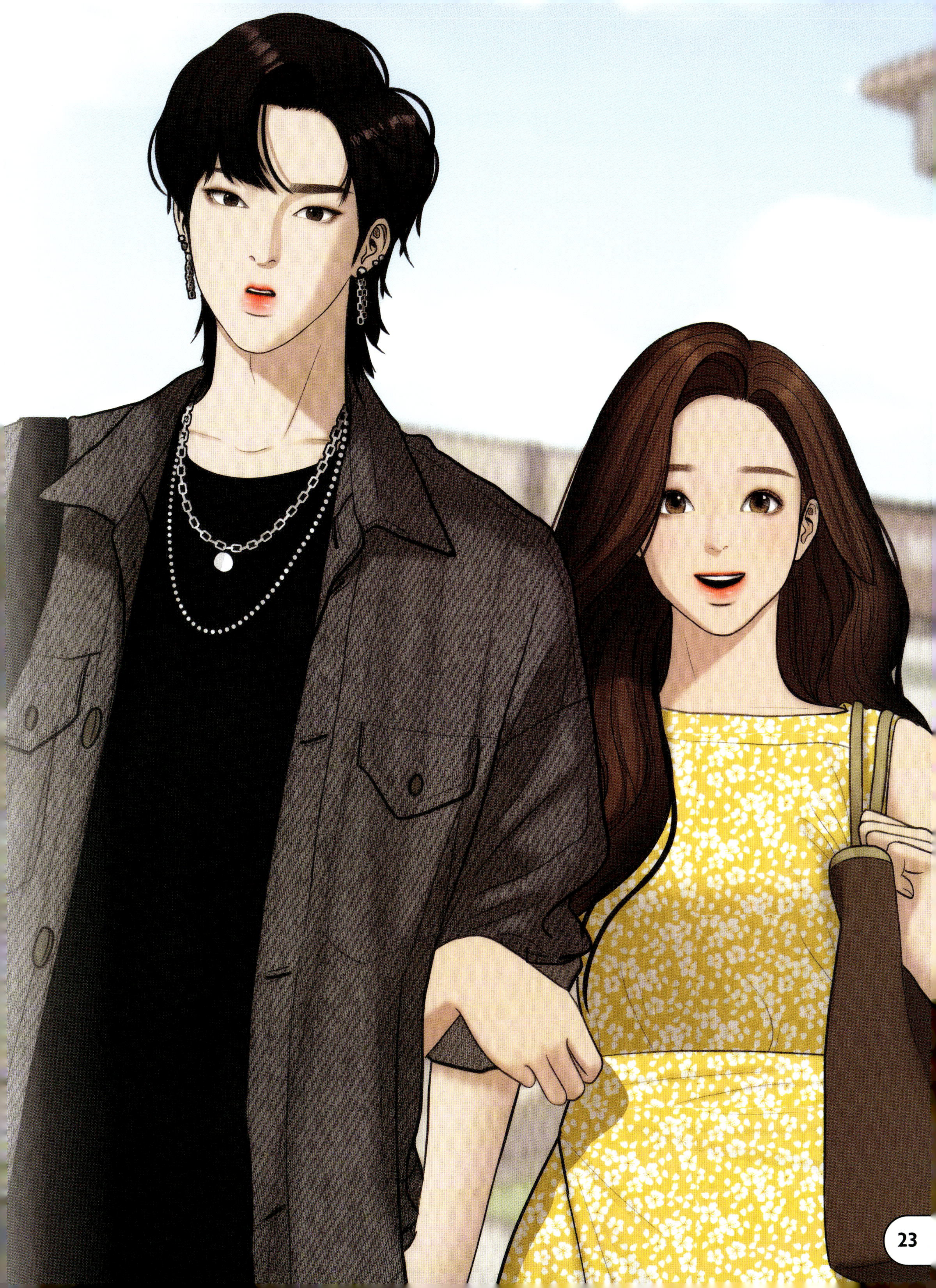

Tools & Materials

Whether you are sketching on paper or drawing digitally, there are some basic tools that will help you on your artistic journey.

Pencils

Graphite pencils come in various densities that help you achieve different shading techniques. The harder or denser the lead is, the lighter it will draw on paper. For a light shade, you can use a 2H pencil. An HB pencil will give you a medium shade, and for darker shades, you can use between 2B and 6B pencils. If you are a beginner artist, start with an HB pencil. Try different pencils and see which one works best for you.

Erasers

When cleaning up your sketches, try using a good-quality rubber or vinyl eraser. You don't want something that will smudge your artwork as you are removing guidelines. A kneaded eraser is also a great tool and is a very pliable and versatile option that won't leave any dust or residue on your paper. You can mold the eraser into any shape to erase precisely.

Pens & Inks

Fine-line markers come in different widths and are easy to use. Once you have finalized your sketches, it's great to go back and finish with a clean, sharp line. Make sure to use permanent ink markers so they won't smudge when adding color or erasing pencil lines. If you want variety in your pen strokes, try using a brush pen. The more pressure you use with a brush pen, the thicker the lines. Light pressure is perfect for very fine details.

Adding Color

Colored pencils are great for adding shading and depth to your drawings. Make sure to sharpen them when using them for detail work.

Markers are perfect for adding large areas of color. Make sure to draw your strokes in quick succession to help them look smooth and blended. Add details or shading on top by letting your strokes dry first and then building up the color. Watercolor paints are also a great medium to use to add color to your inked drawings.

Paper

A sketchbook is a great tool. Always have your sketchbook handy when developing your art practice. They come in a variety of sizes and shapes. A good mixed-media sketchbook is a great place to start. If you are using paints or markers, choose a thicker paper so the wet media doesn't bleed through.

Digital Tools

Webcomics are created digitally, so it is great to familiarize yourself with digital drawing tools. There are many different drawing apps available at a low cost; some are even free. Drawing tablets with pens can be used for digital drawing. There are many to choose from, so research and test out your options to find the right tablet for you. I use Adobe Photoshop and a digital tablet for most of my work.

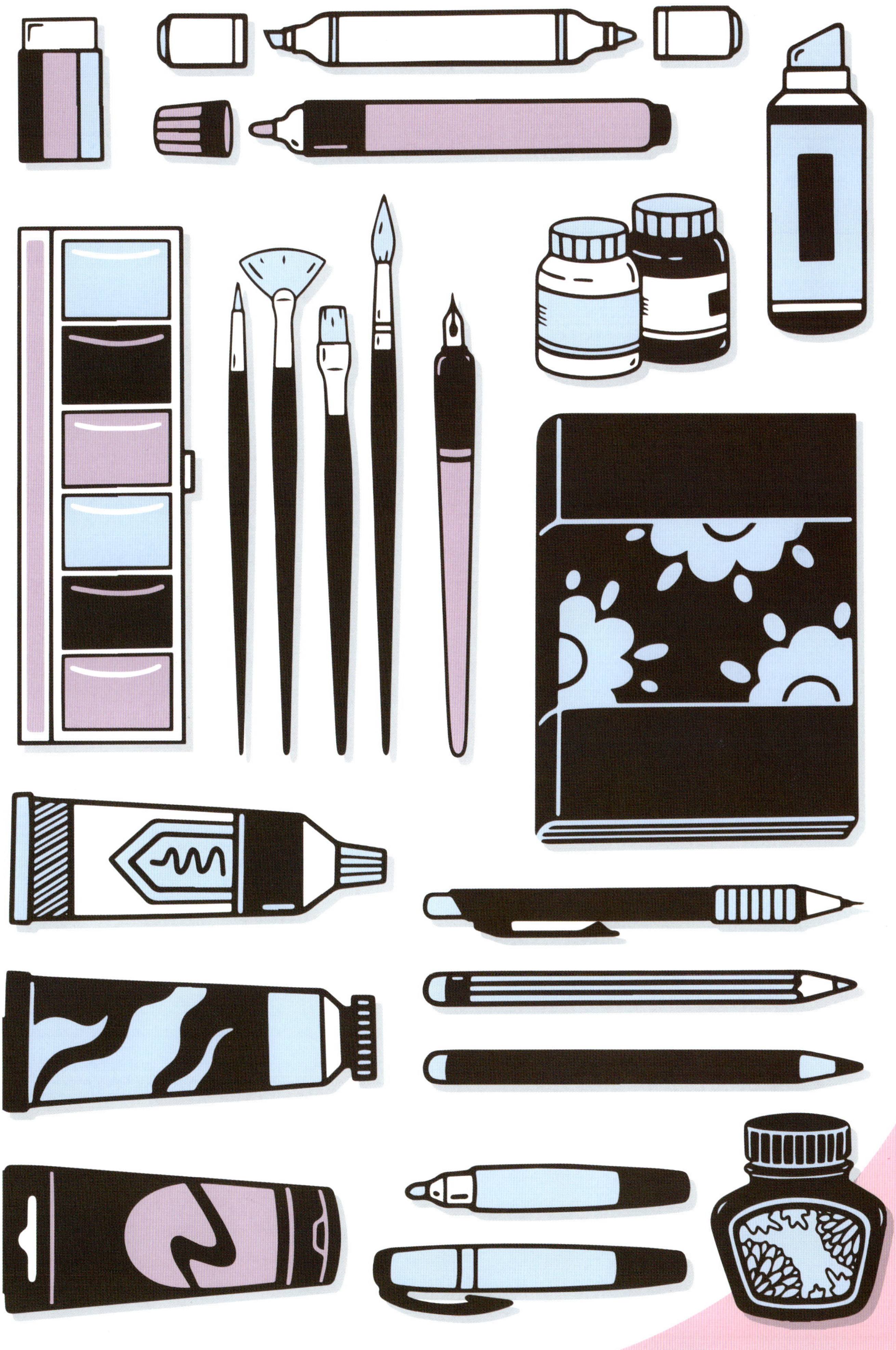

Anatomy Basics: Head & Face

It's important to have a solid grasp of the basics when drawing people and characters. A good way to start learning how to draw three-dimensional figures in two-dimensional spaces is to learn basic human anatomy.

Basic Face Shape Proportions

The head can be divided into standard proportions to help guide you in drawing faces. The eyes are positioned halfway between the top of the head and the tip of the chin. The tip of the nose is located approximately halfway between the eyeline and the chin. Keep in mind that proportions can vary based on several factors, including age, ethnicity, and gender.

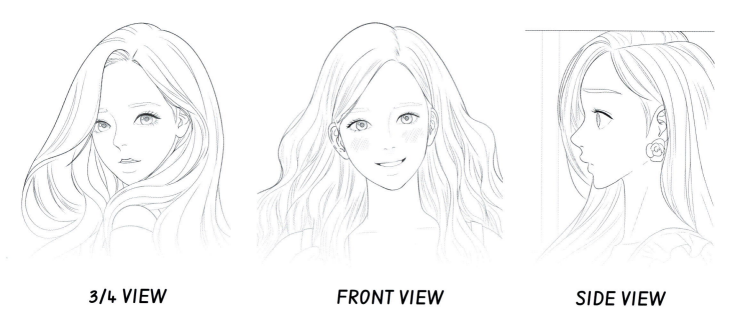

3/4 VIEW   FRONT VIEW   SIDE VIEW

Face Views

There are three basic views of the head and face: the front view, the three-quarter (3/4) view, and the side view. When the head is kept level, the horizontal guidelines stay the same. When the chin tilts up or down, the horizontal guidelines curve with the form of the head.

Eyes & Emotion

As a webcomic artist, you must be able to communicate a lot of action in a small frame, so it's important that the eyes register emotions that match a character's mood and expression in addition to the aligning with the story.

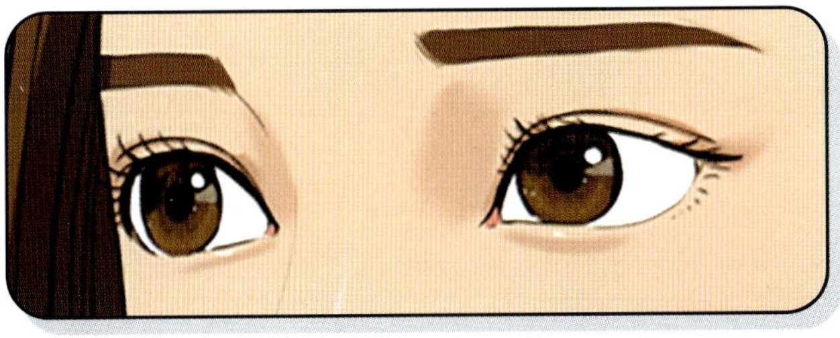

Neutral eyes show a character who is listening or observing or doesn't have a strong opinion.

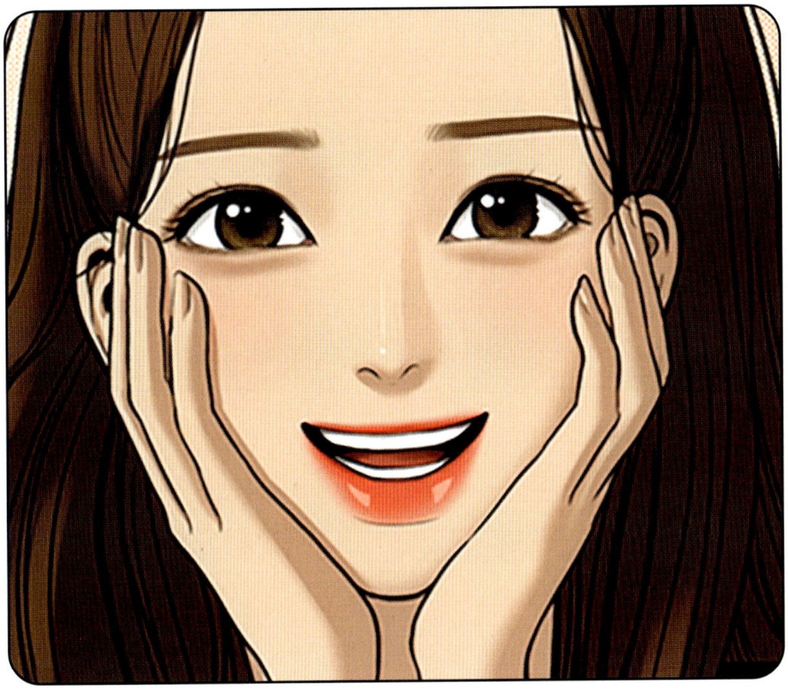

Soft eyes indicate a relaxed or happy mood.

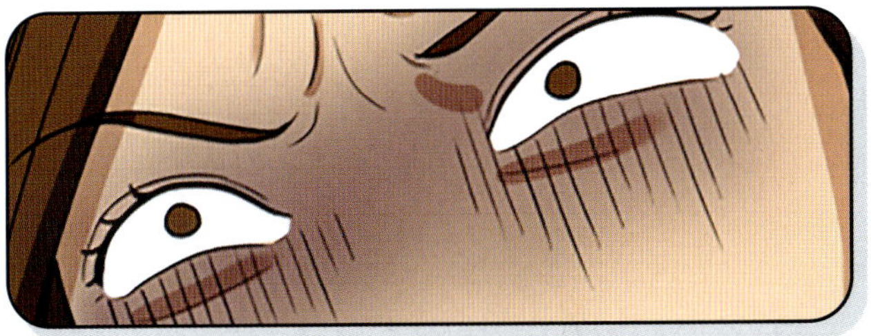

Narrowed eyes show intensity or anger.

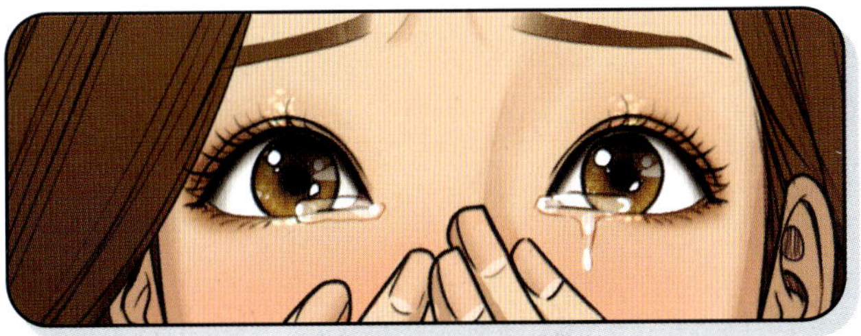

Watery eyes generally show joy or sorrow.

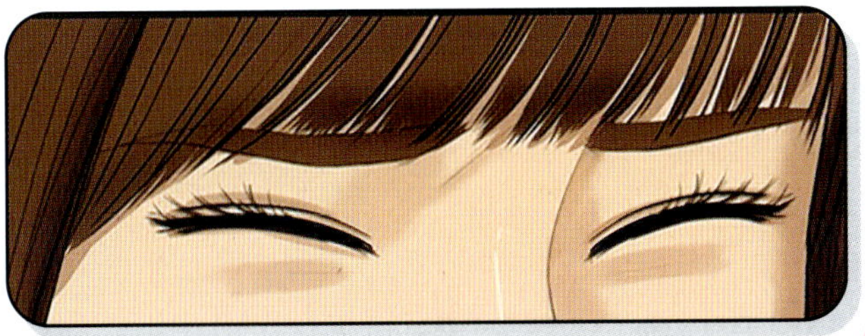

Eyes squeezed shut can show excitement or anticipation.

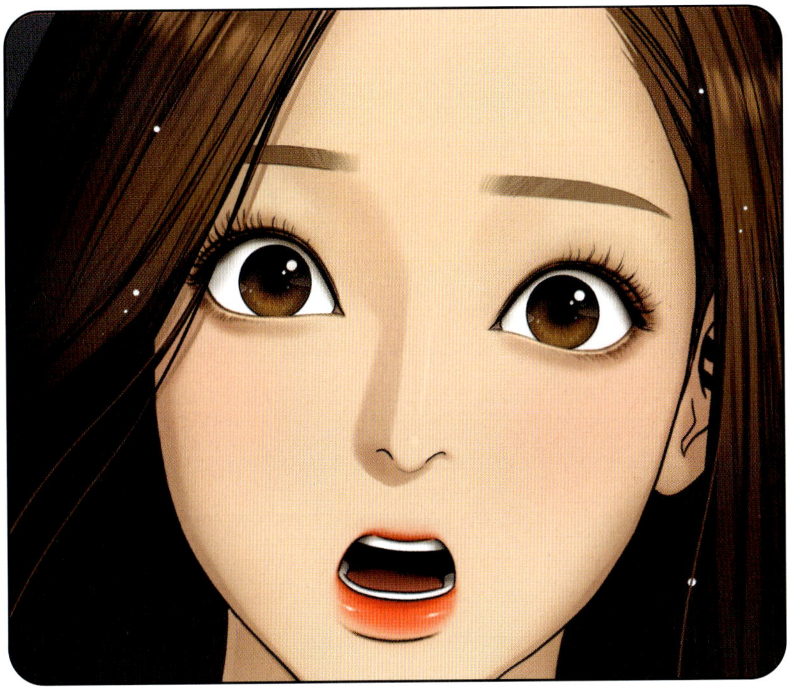

Wide eyes register surprise or shock.

Expressions

Expressions are important because they help convey a character's mood and motivation while also contributing to the action of each scene. When you draw your characters, try to emphasize a specific mood or action without worrying about following normal facial proportions. Have fun exaggerating the features to create different emotions.

Annoyed

Indecisive

Confident

Smitten

Adorable

Exhausted

Excited

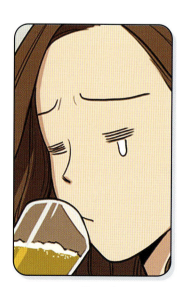
Sad

Furrowed eyebrows, wide eyes

Open mouth

Worried

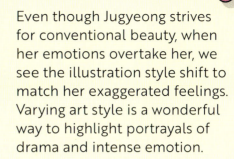

Even though Jugyeong strives for conventional beauty, when her emotions overtake her, we see the illustration style shift to match her exaggerated feelings. Varying art style is a wonderful way to highlight portrayals of drama and intense emotion.

Once you have a character's facial proportions down, it's fairly simple to adjust the expression. Start with a neutral face like the one shown. Then play around with the eyes, eyebrows, and mouth to create different looks. Use your color tools to emphasize your character's features, such as the eyes and mouth.

Anatomy Basics: Body

One of the keys to drawing successful believable bodies is to gain an understanding of basic human proportions (how the size of each body part relates to the whole body). However, think of these proportions as guidelines. Your characters' proportions might vary depending on their unique qualities.

Height is generally measured in head size, which means each section of the body is roughly the same size as the head. Most adult bodies are between six and eight heads tall. Use this as a general guide, but know that some characters might be shorter or taller. Chibi characters, for example, are usually only two to three heads tall.

Dividing the body into segments according to the size of the head is a helpful tool for mastering proportion.

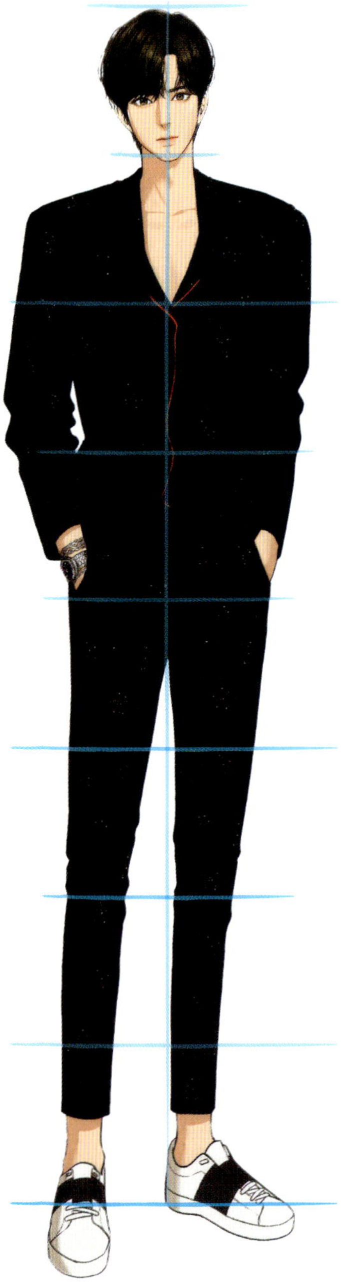

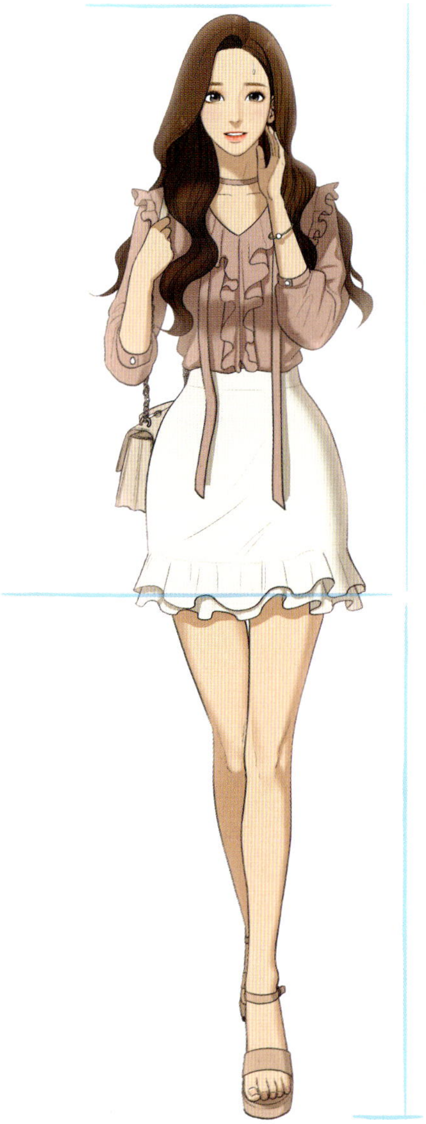

Another helpful measurement is to divide the figure in half. The distance from the top of the head to the top of the thigh is about the same as the distance between the top of the thigh and the bottom of the feet.

Body Positions

Once you have an understanding of the basic proportions, start examining how specific parts of the body move and bend. It's helpful to think about the body in terms of volume and shape versus in flat two-dimensional images. Try to maintain the natural proportions of the body even when it's in a twisted or seated position.

When the body moves, the vertical and horizontal axis lines also move. Notice how the chest, neck, face, and pelvis won't always face the same direction. Becoming familiar with the body's movements will help your character poses look natural.

A character in the seated position will often have softer shoulders and a more relaxed demeanor.

Movement & Emotions

Emotion is communicated through whole-body movement in addition to facial expressions. Together, expression and movement convey a character's reaction, mood, or motivation. Sometimes, the body can tell the story by itself even when a face is concealed.

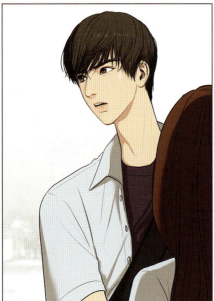

Body language and facial expressions can add to a story without the use of dialogue or narration. In this scene, one character is pulled out of the path of an oncoming motorcycle. How do the facial expressions and body positions tell this story?

When it comes to a character's emotions, the hands help tell the story in combination with facial expressions and body position.

An extended arm combined with a pointing finger communicates a tone that might be accusatory or aggressive in nature. How does the facial expression and a hand on the hip further contribute to this character's emotional state?

Hands covering the face can communicate embarrassment, sadness, or despair.

A firm grip can indicate tension in a scene, especially when one character has their grip on another.

Body language can add to a story without the use of dialogue.

33

DRAWING STEP-BY-STEP

Learn to draw your favorite *True Beauty* Characters.

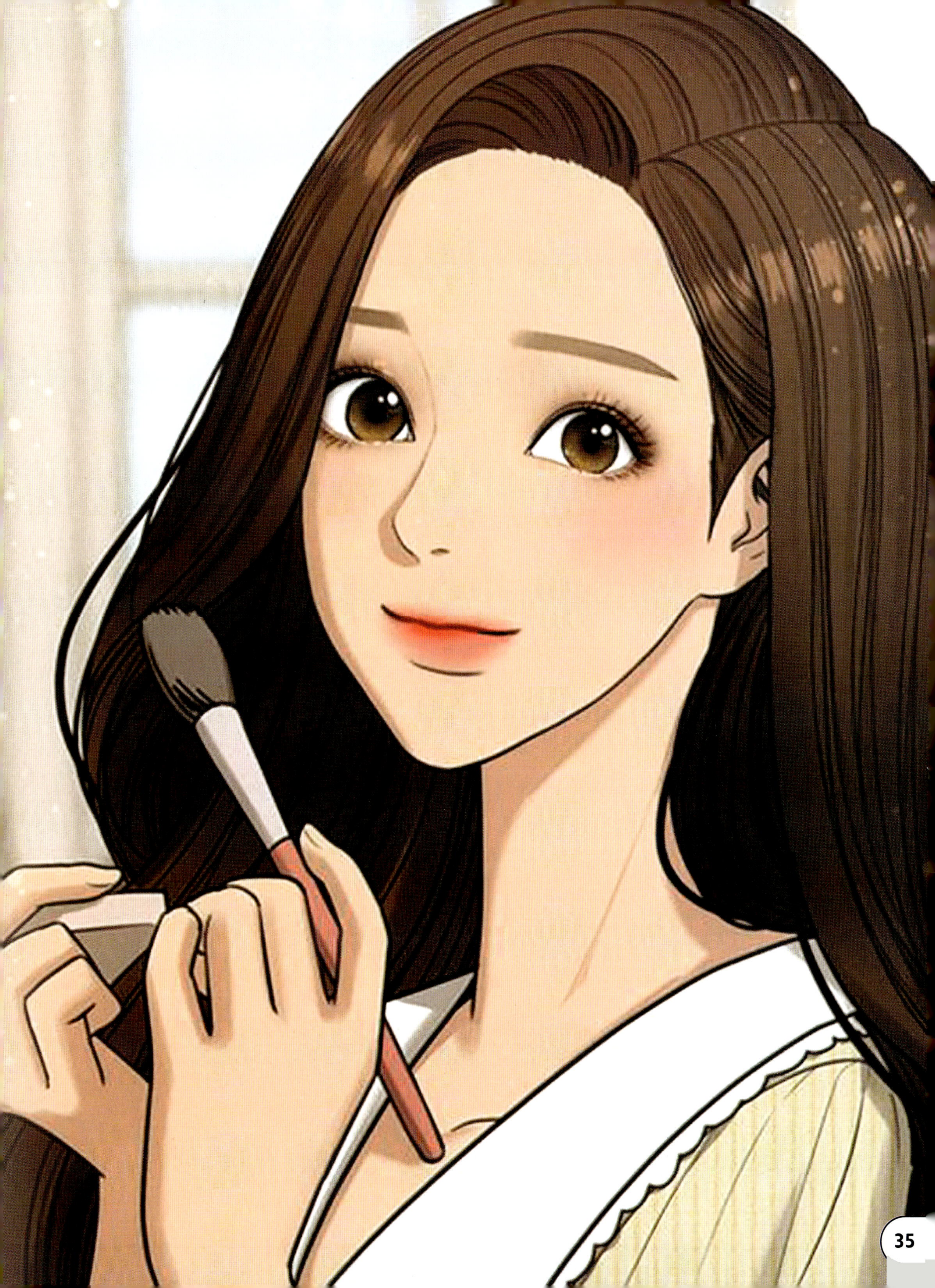

Jugyeong
Natural (Front View)

Start with a circle and guidelines to help place the facial features. Next, rough in the shape of the figure. Begin to fill in the face, adding the eyes, nose, and mouth. Continue to add the details until you are happy with your drawing. Erase old sketch lines and then color your art.

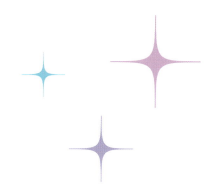
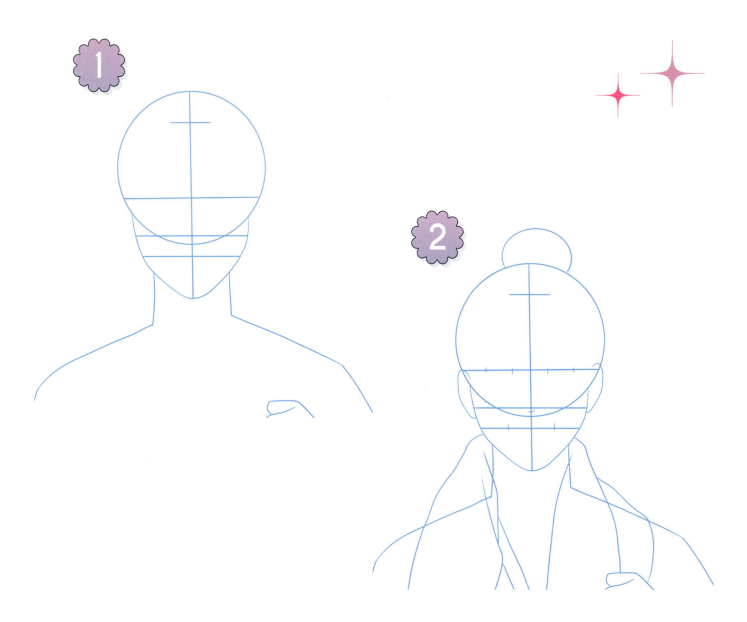

3

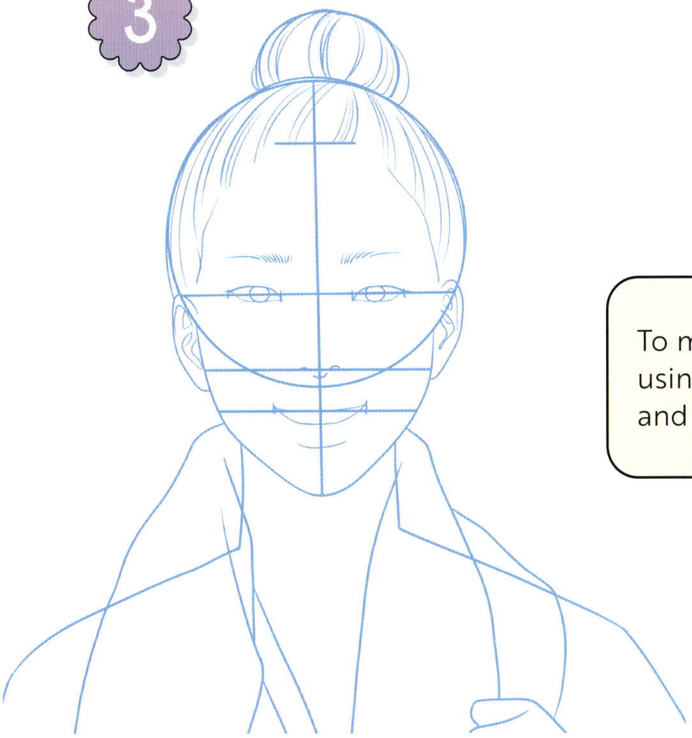

To make this art your own, experiment using different color palettes, poses, and outfits in your drawings.

4

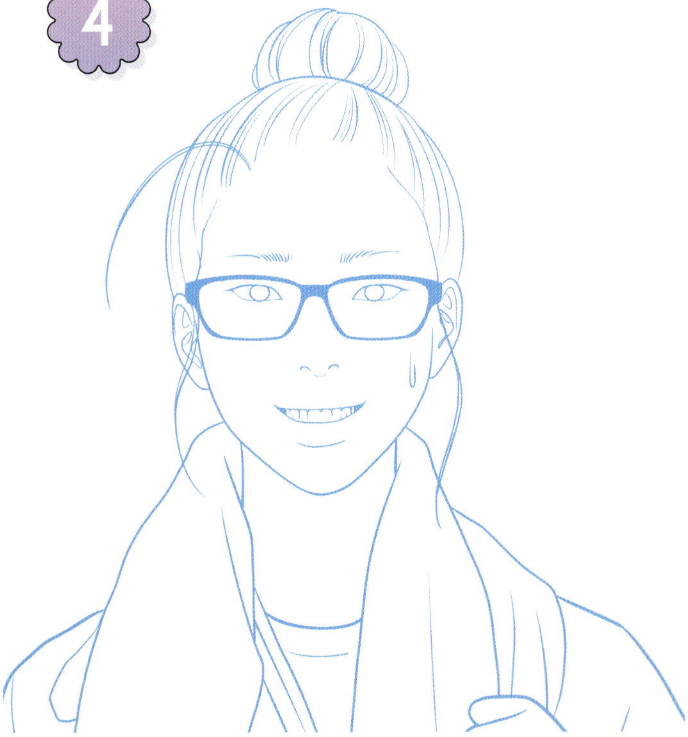

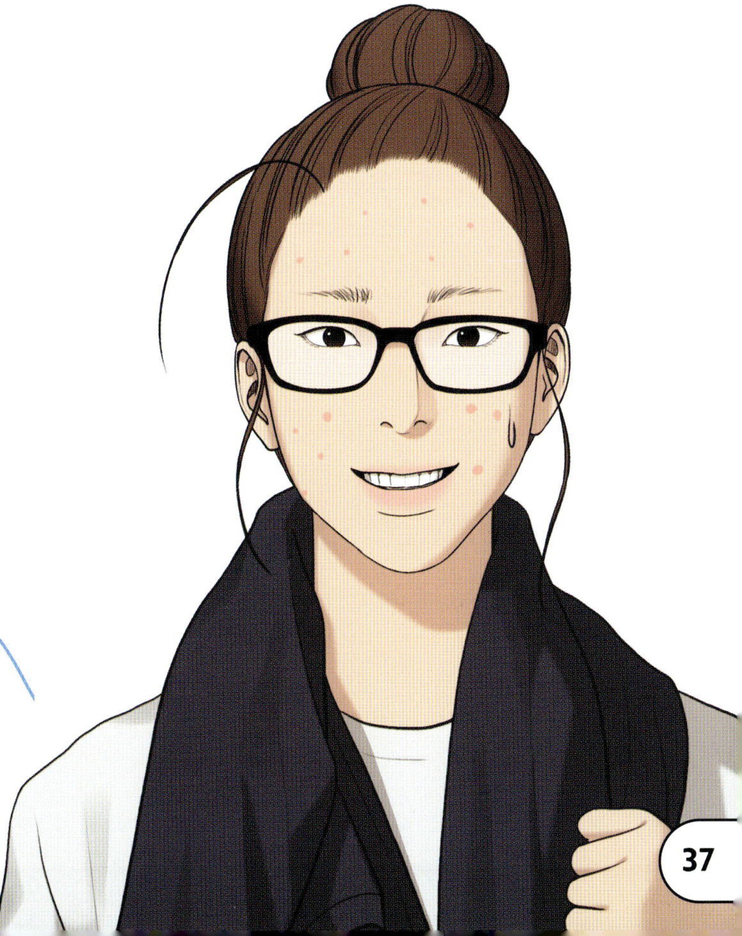

Jugyeong
Makeup (Front View)

Start with a circle and guidelines to help place the facial features. This face is tilted so make sure to adjust your guidelines accordingly. Rough in the shape of the figure and begin to fill in the details. Draw eyes, nose, and mouth. Erase old sketch lines and then add color using the tools of your choice.

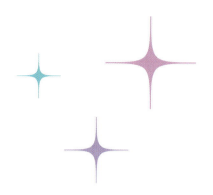

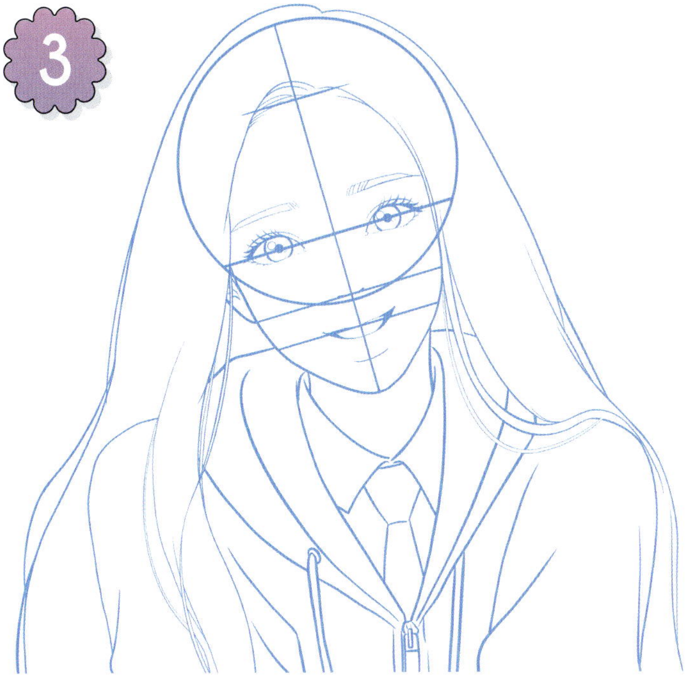
3

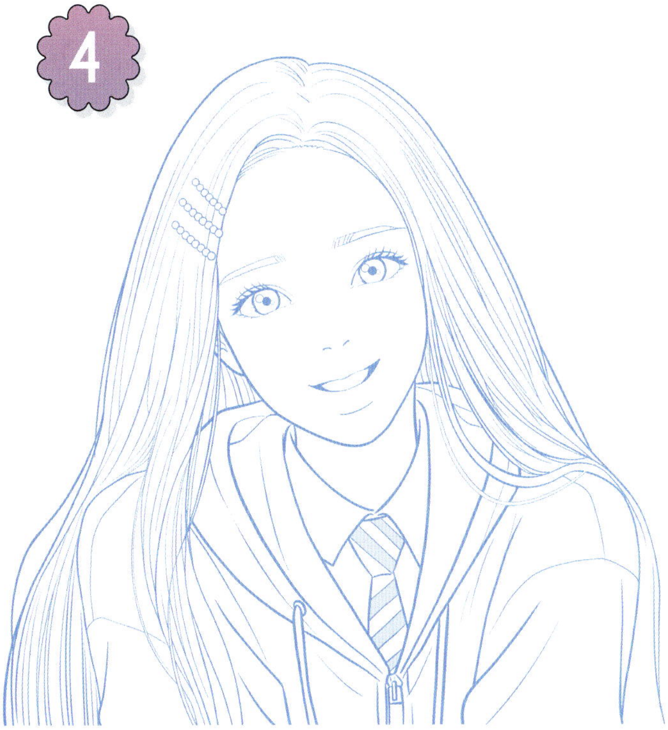
4

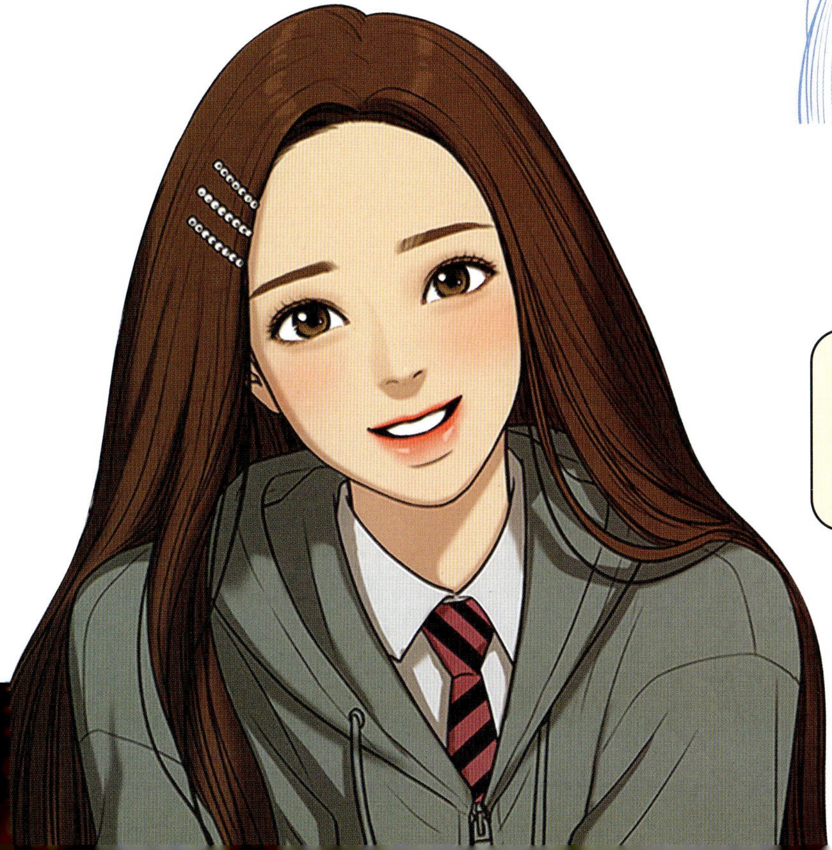

Jugyeong's makeup is soft and muted. Use shades of coral and peach to give her skin a soft glow.

Jugyeong
Natural & Makeup Split (Front View)

This unique pose features Jugyeong split between her natural self and made-up self. Start with a circle for the head. Then add a vertical line to represent both the spine and the split. Add broad geometrical shapes for the body and circles for the joints. Continue to add the details until you are happy with your drawing.

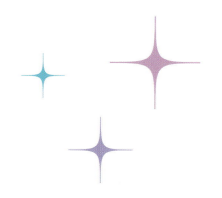

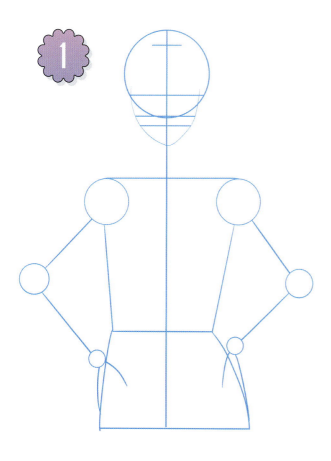

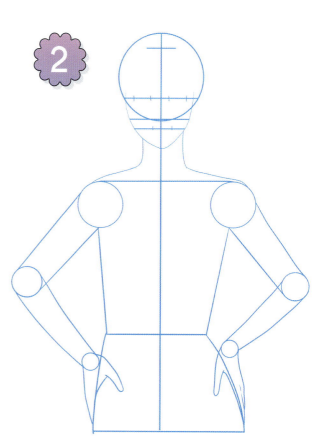

3

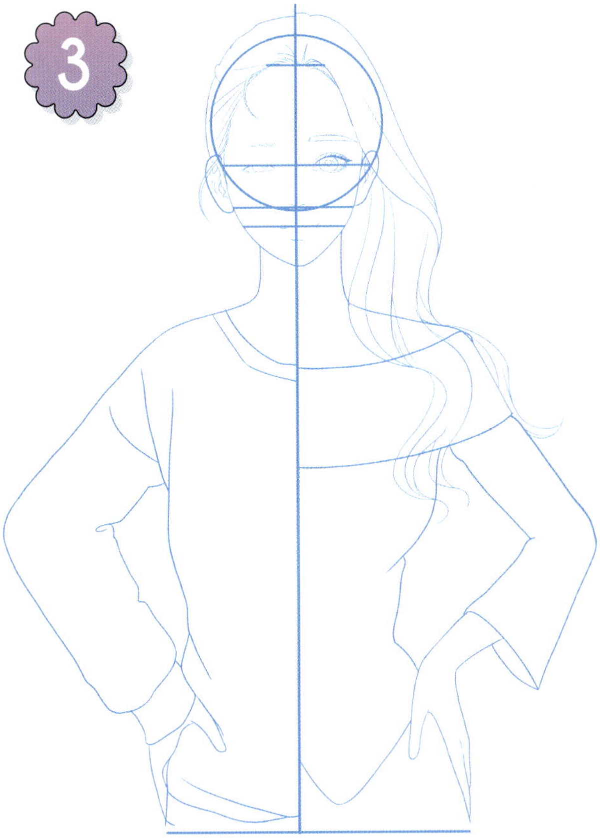

4

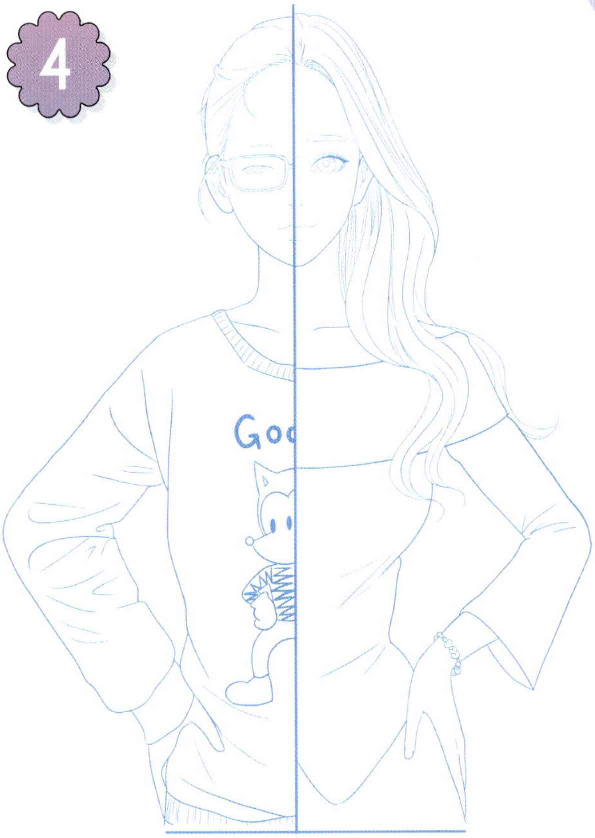

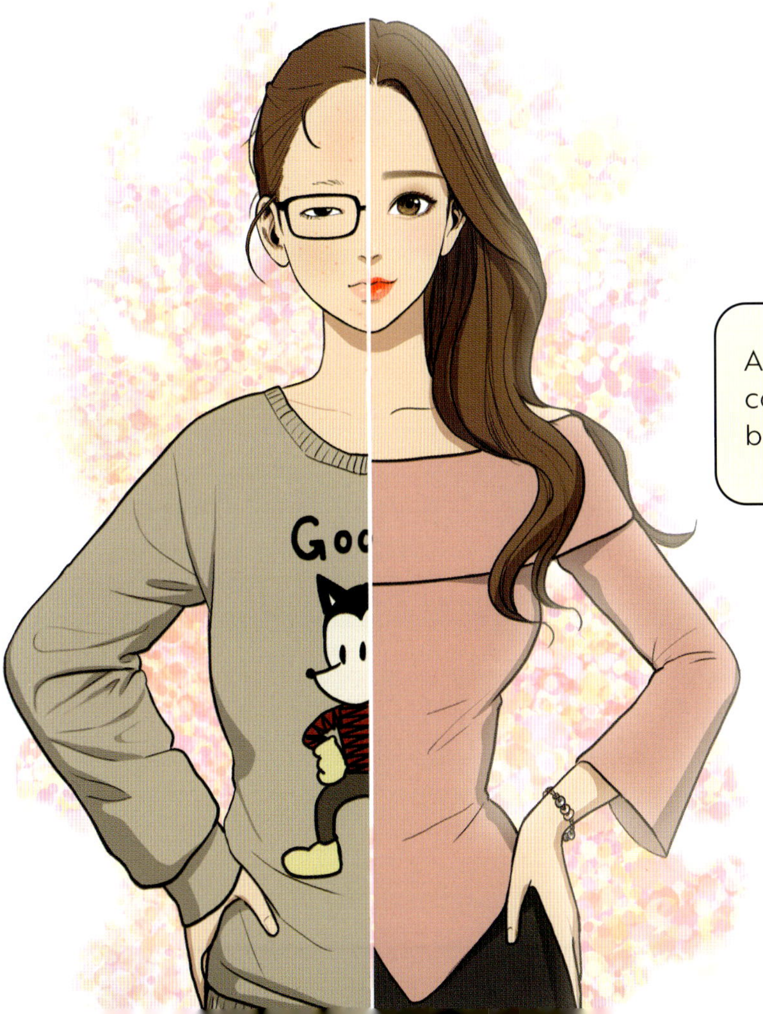

Add some dabs of pink, peach, and coral to create a mottled background behind Jugyeong.

Jugyeong
Body (Front View)

Start with a circle for the head. Then add a vertical line to represent the spine. Add broad geometrical shapes for the body, lines for the limbs, and circles for the joints. Continue to fill in the details. Take extra time finessing the ruffles on the blouse and skirt so that the lines flow and the look is natural. Erase any old sketch lines and add color.

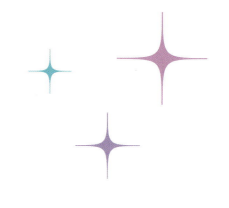

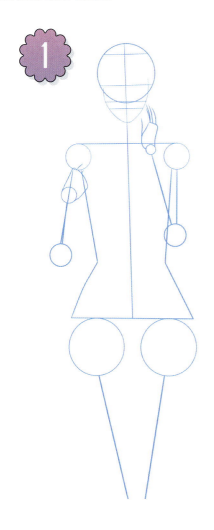

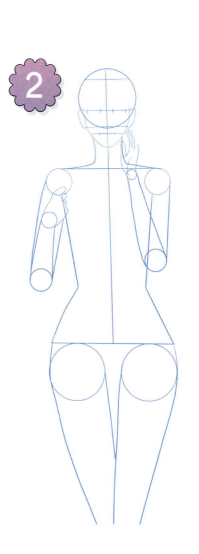

3

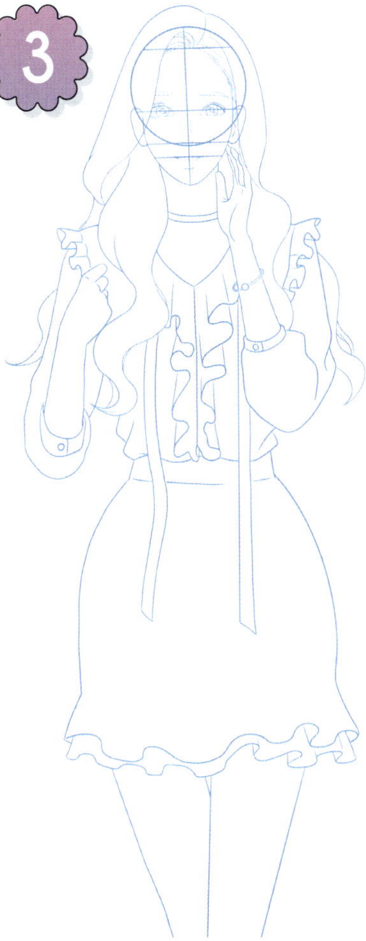

Include subtle details, including lines to show fabric wrinkles and shading to add dimension.

4

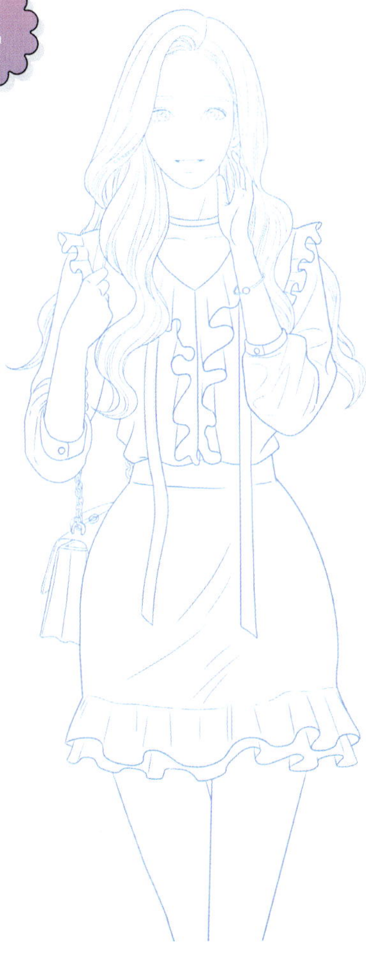

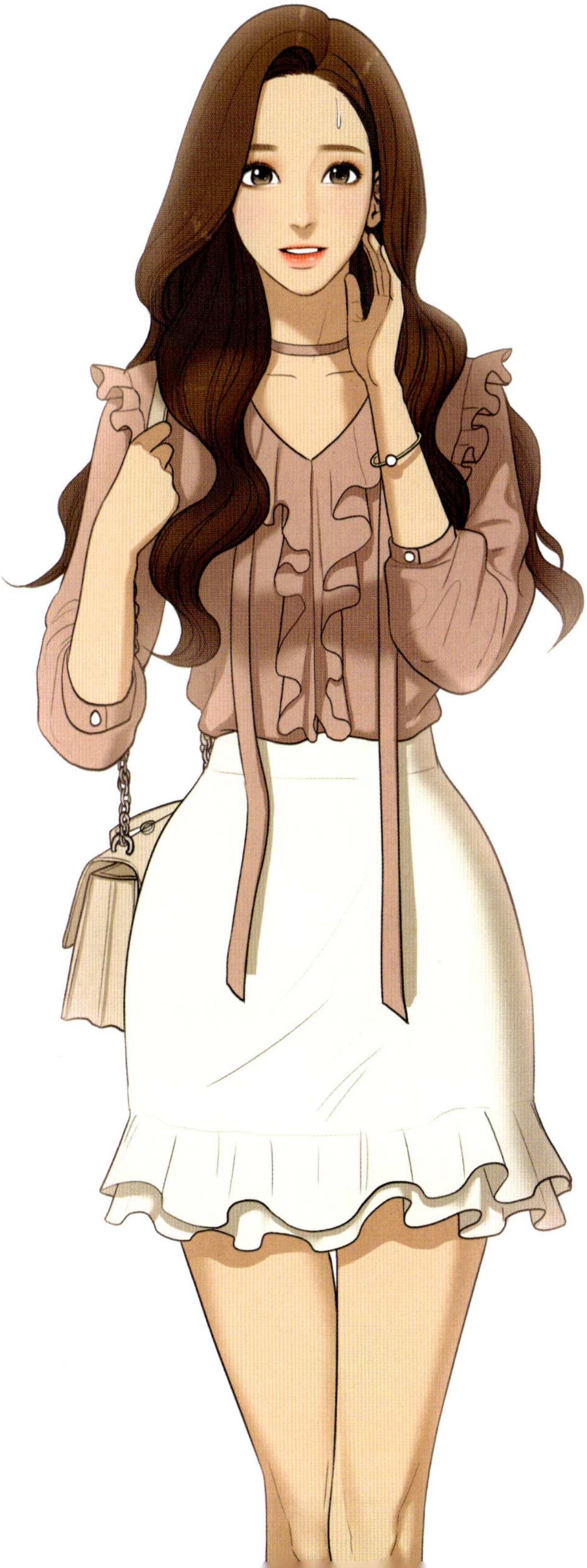

Jugyeong

Body (3/4 View)

Start with a circle for the head. Then add a vertical line to represent the spine. Add broad geometrical shapes for the body, lines for the limbs, and circles for the joints. At this stage, the body still looks flat. As you begin to fill in the details, notice how the form begins to fill out and take shape.

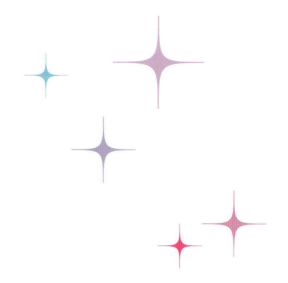

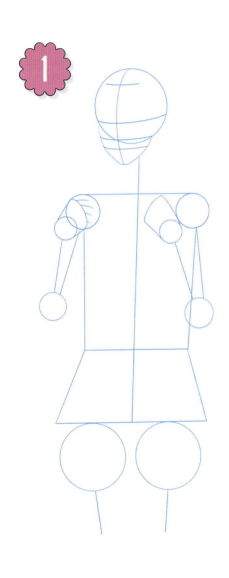

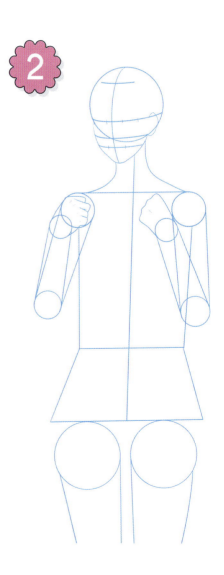

3

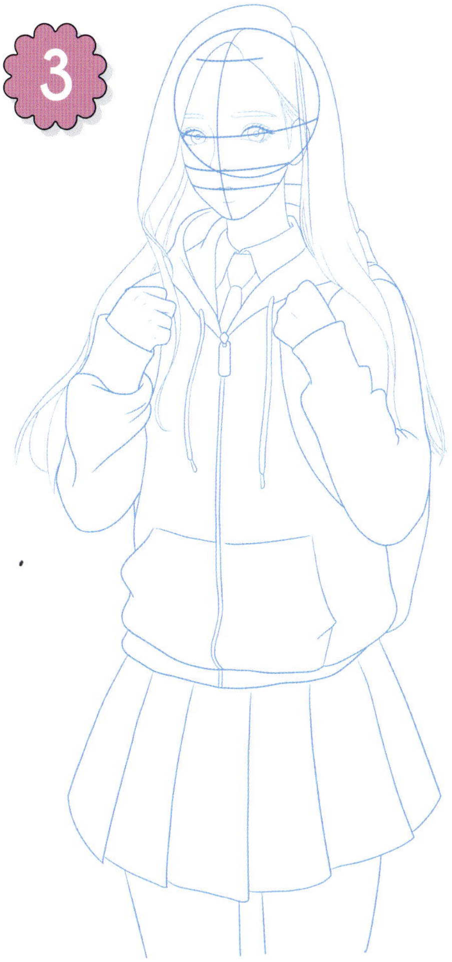

When drawing a figure wearing layers of clothing, it's important to start the frame using lines and geometrical shapes. Otherwise, your final figure might look out of proportion.

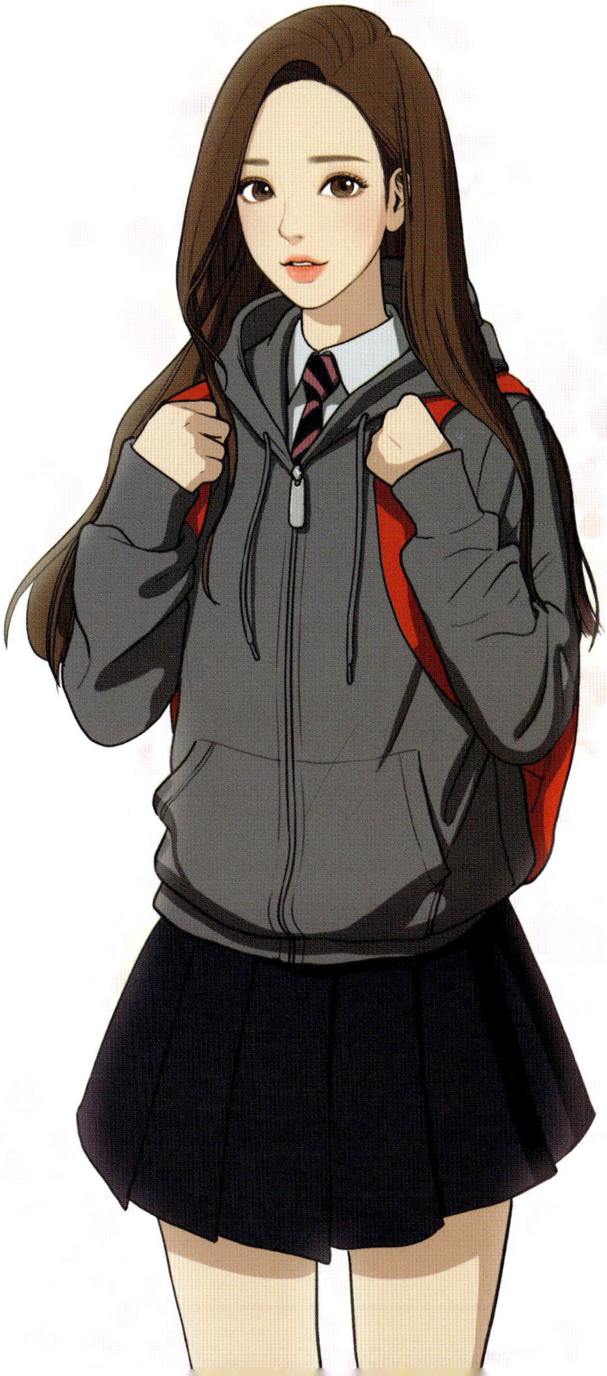

4

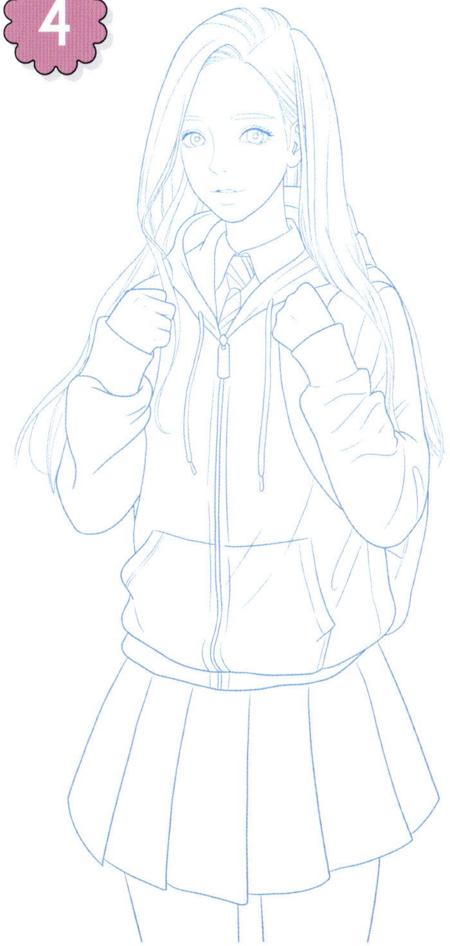

Jugyeong

Front View (with bangs)

Start with a circle for the head and add guidelines to the face. Use lines to establish the basic frame; add circles to denote the joints. Fill in the shape and add the eyes, nose, and mouth to the guidelines. Follow the steps to complete your drawing, and erase any old sketch lines before adding color.

Use a series of simple curved lines to create Jugyeong's bangs and then use your color tools to give them their shape.

1

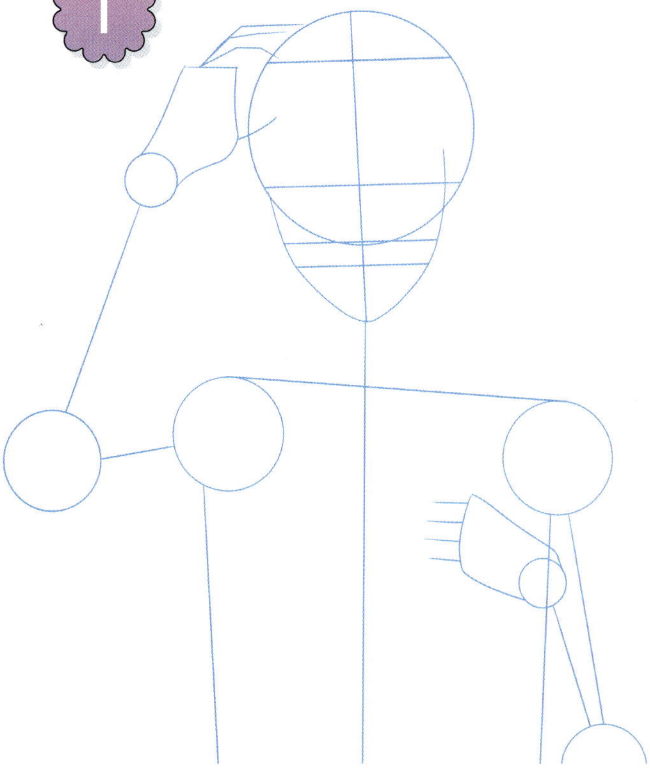

2

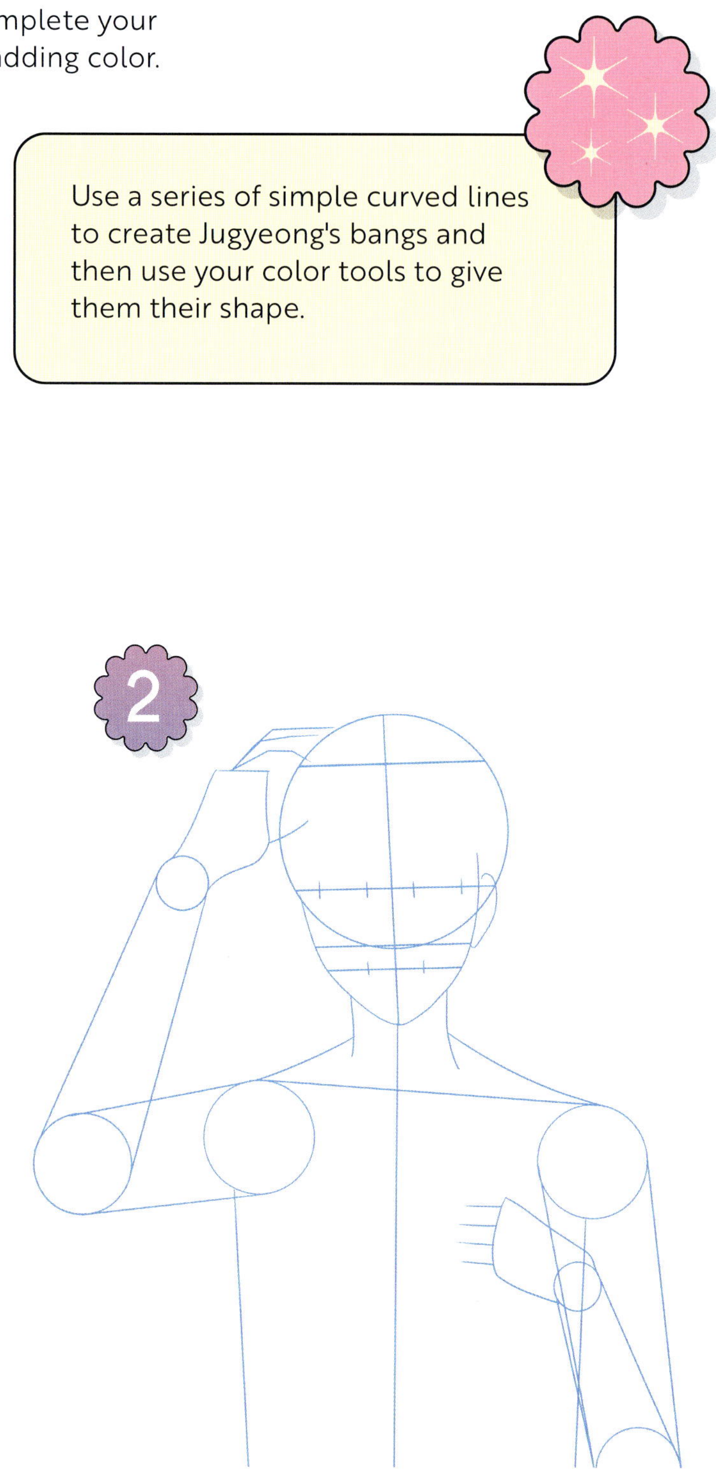

3

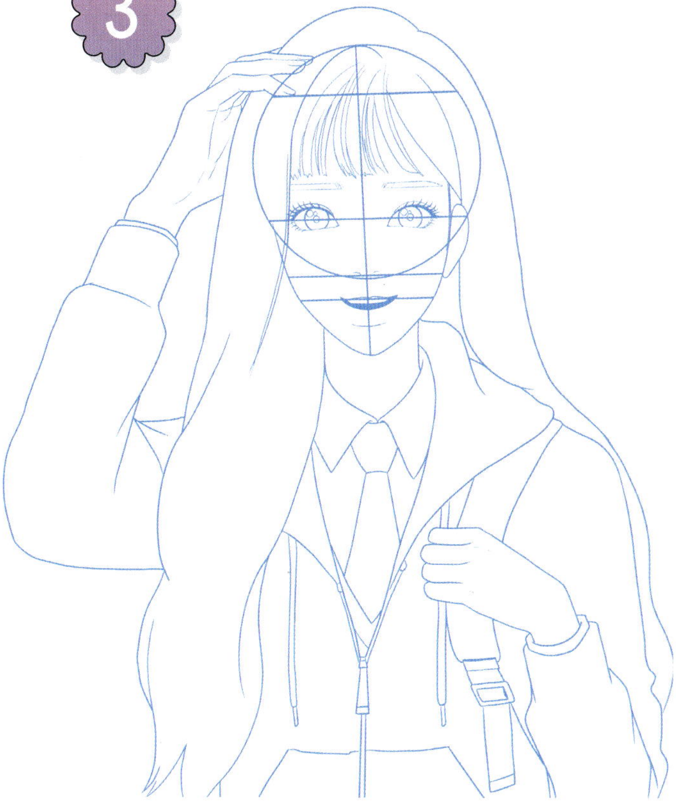

4

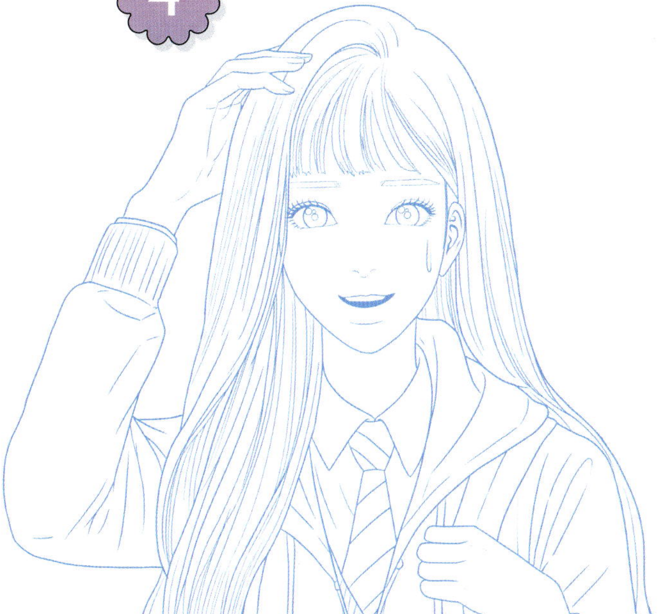

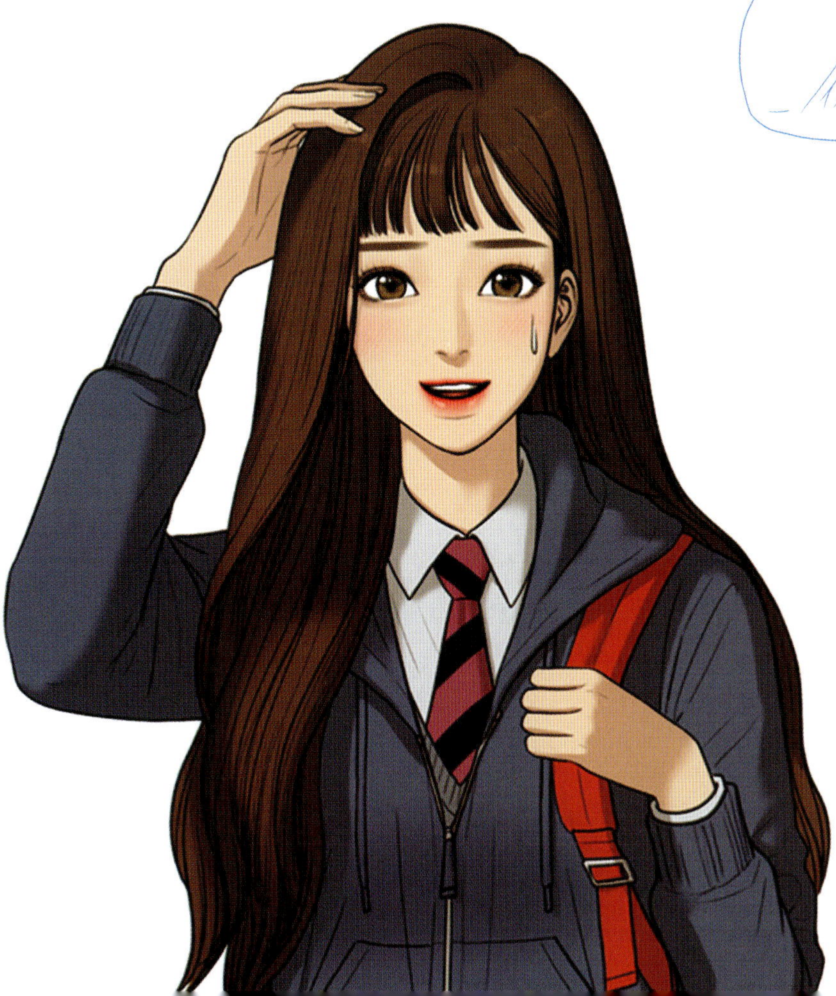

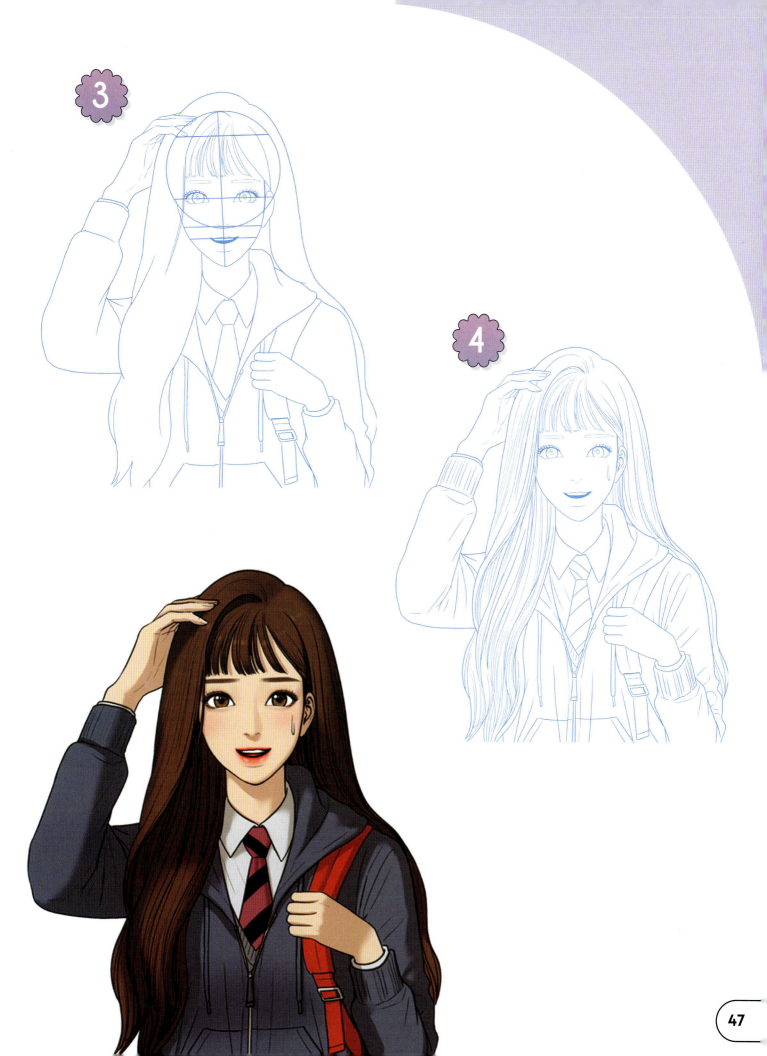

Suho

Head (Front View)

Start with a circle and guidelines to help place the facial features. Next, rough in the shape of the figure. Begin to fill in the details and rough in the eyes, nose, and mouth. Continue to work on the details until you are happy with your drawing. Erase old sketch lines and then color your art.

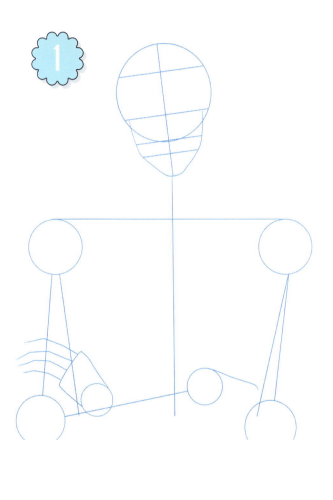

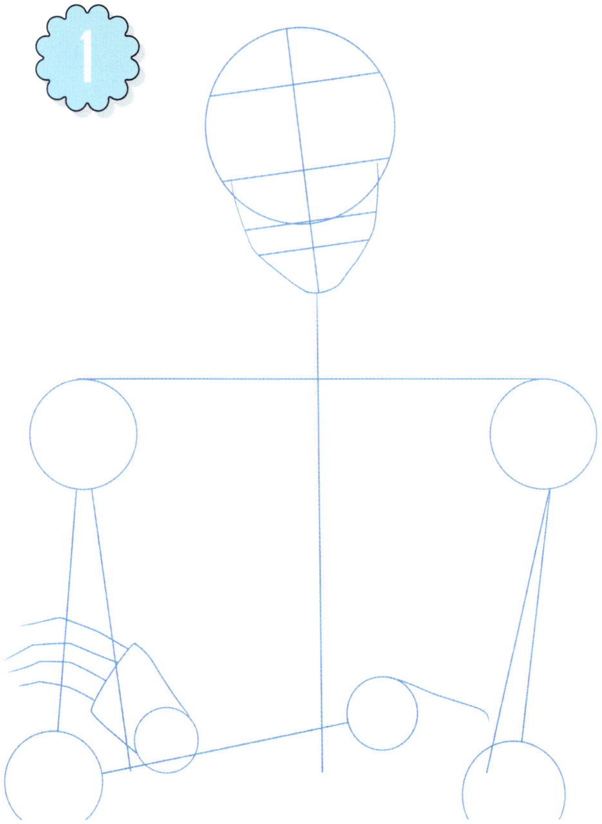

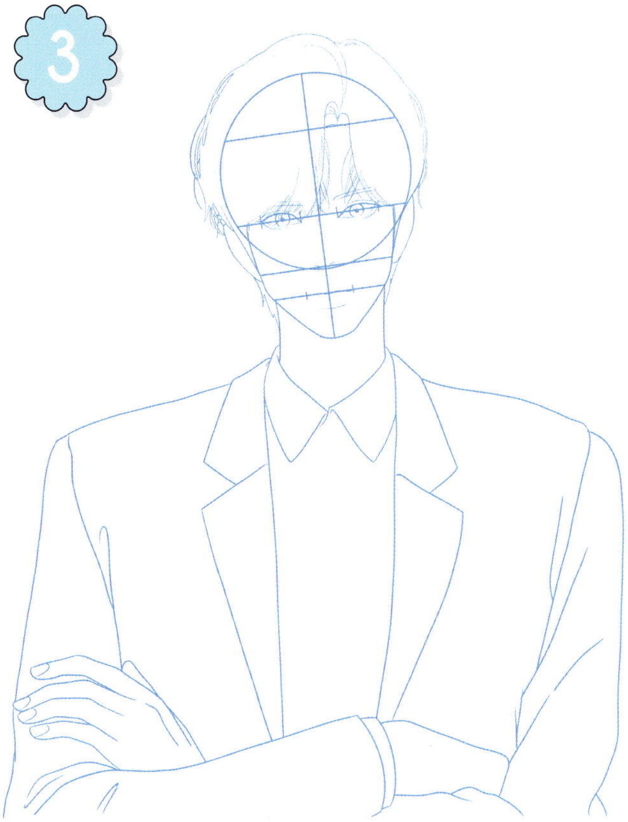
3

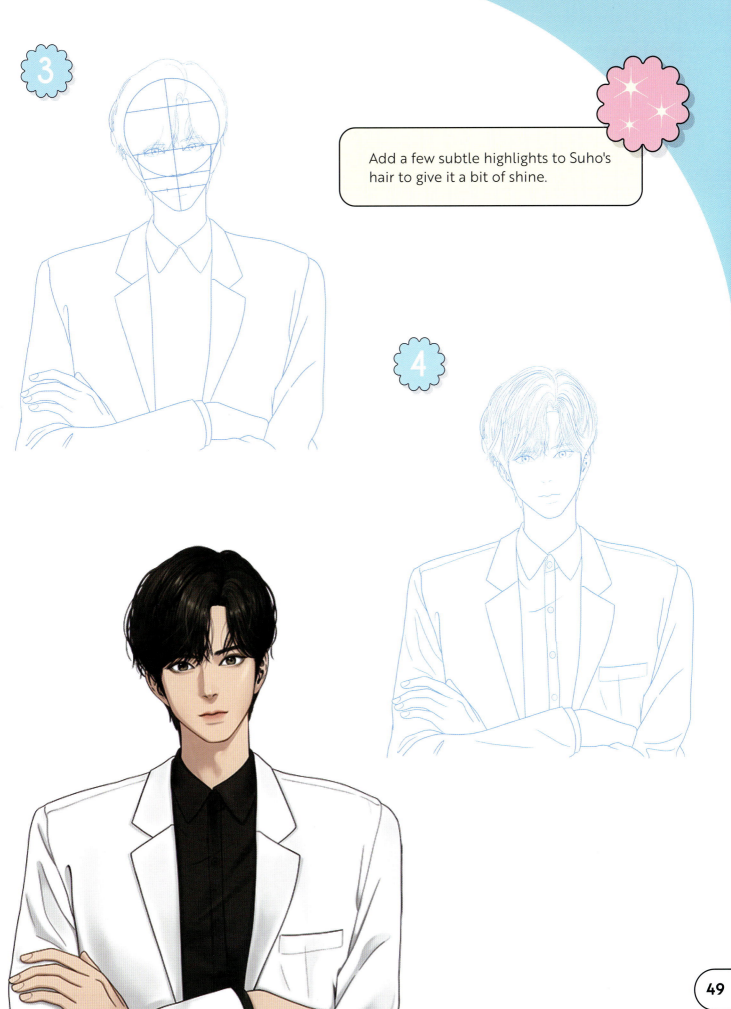

Add a few subtle highlights to Suho's hair to give it a bit of shine.

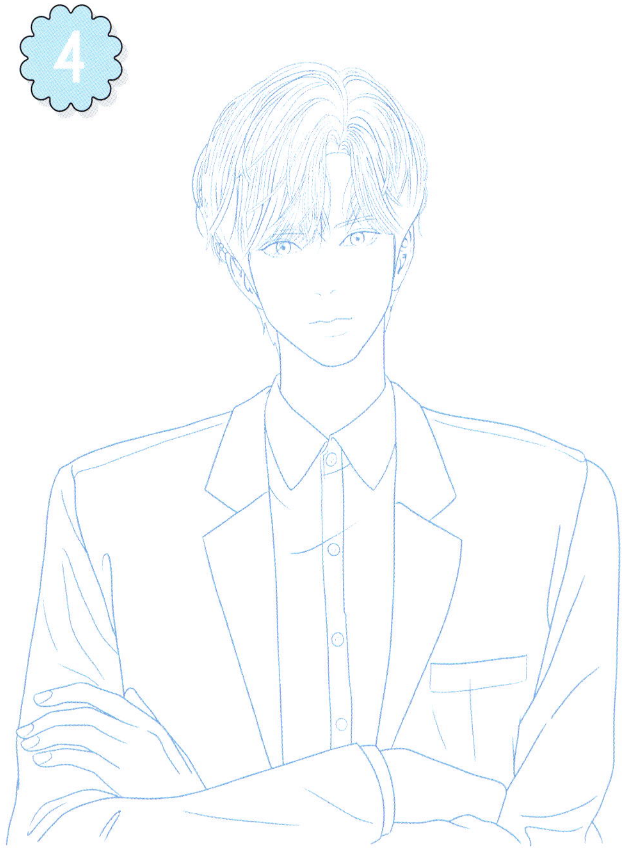
4

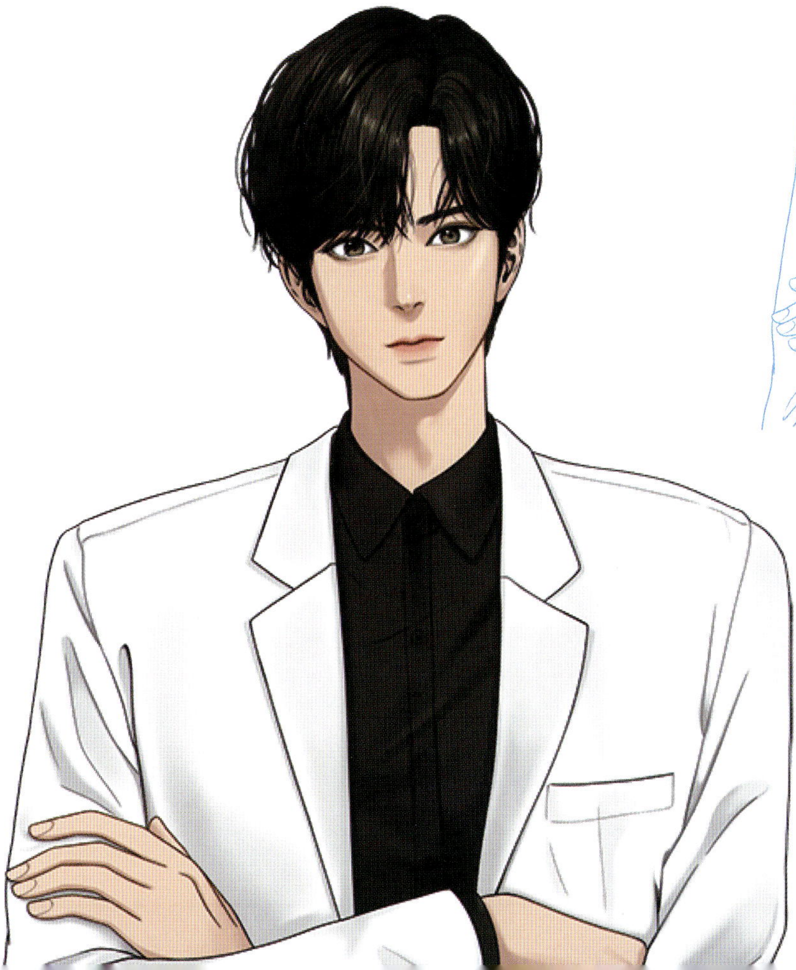

Suho

Body (Front View)

Start with a circle for the head. Then add a vertical line to represent the spine. Add broad geometrical shapes for the body, lines for the limbs, and circles for the joints. Continue to fill in the details.

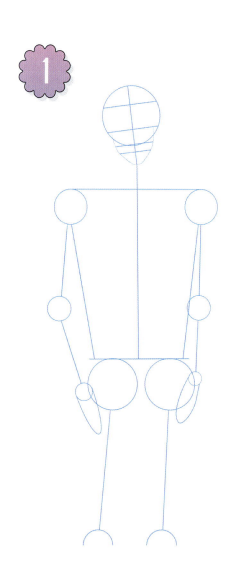

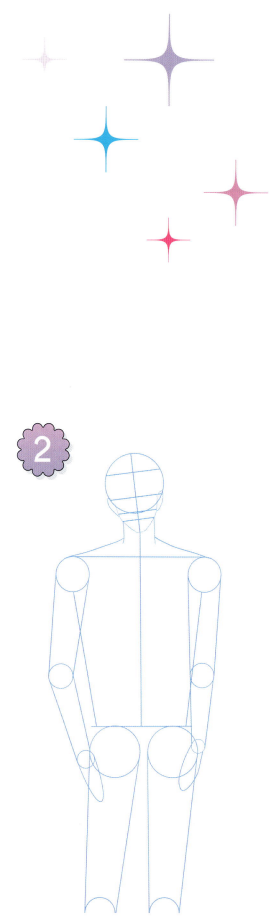

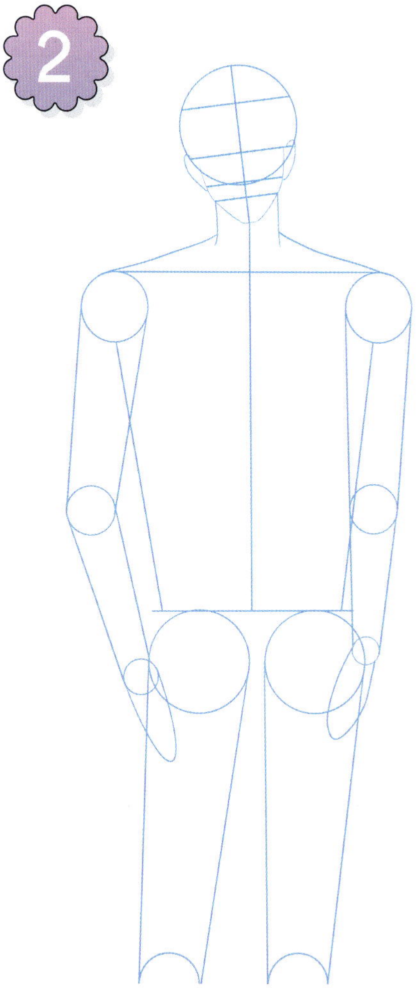

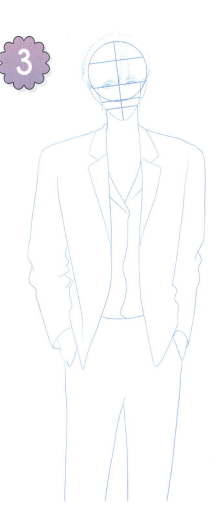

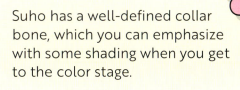

Suho has a well-defined collar bone, which you can emphasize with some shading when you get to the color stage.

Suho

Head (3/4 View)

Start with a circle for the head. Then add a vertical line to represent the neck. Fill in the shape of the chin so it points at an angle, and add guidelines to the face. Continue to follow the steps to complete the drawing.

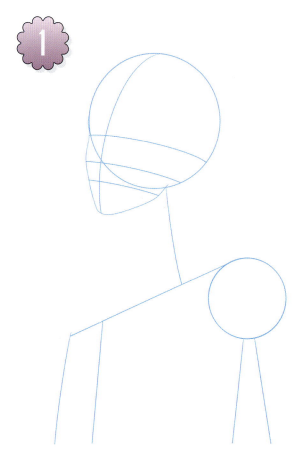

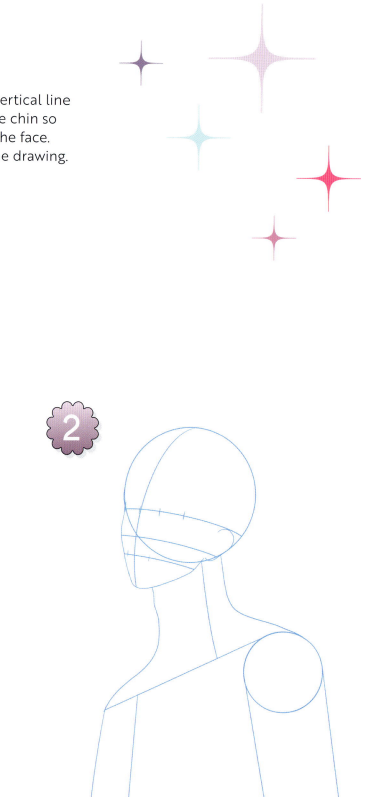

3

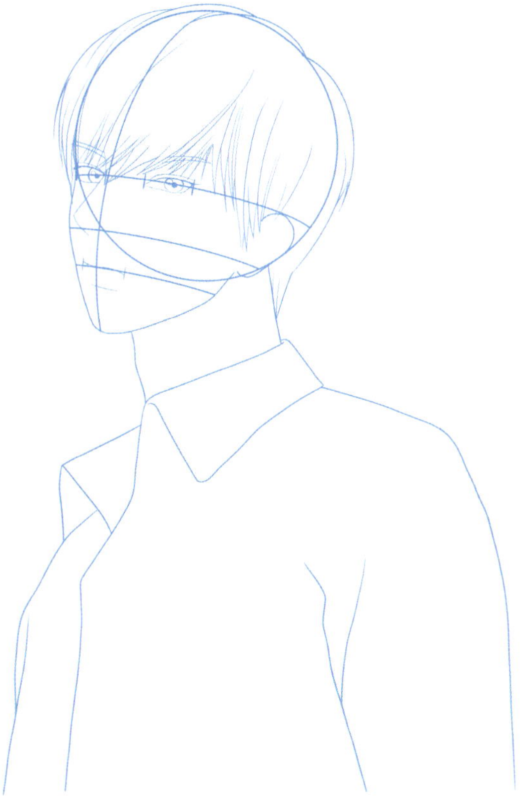

4

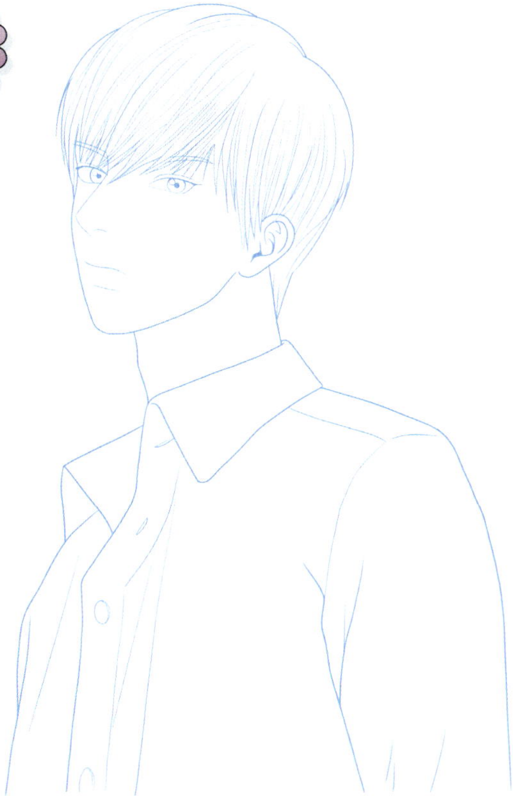

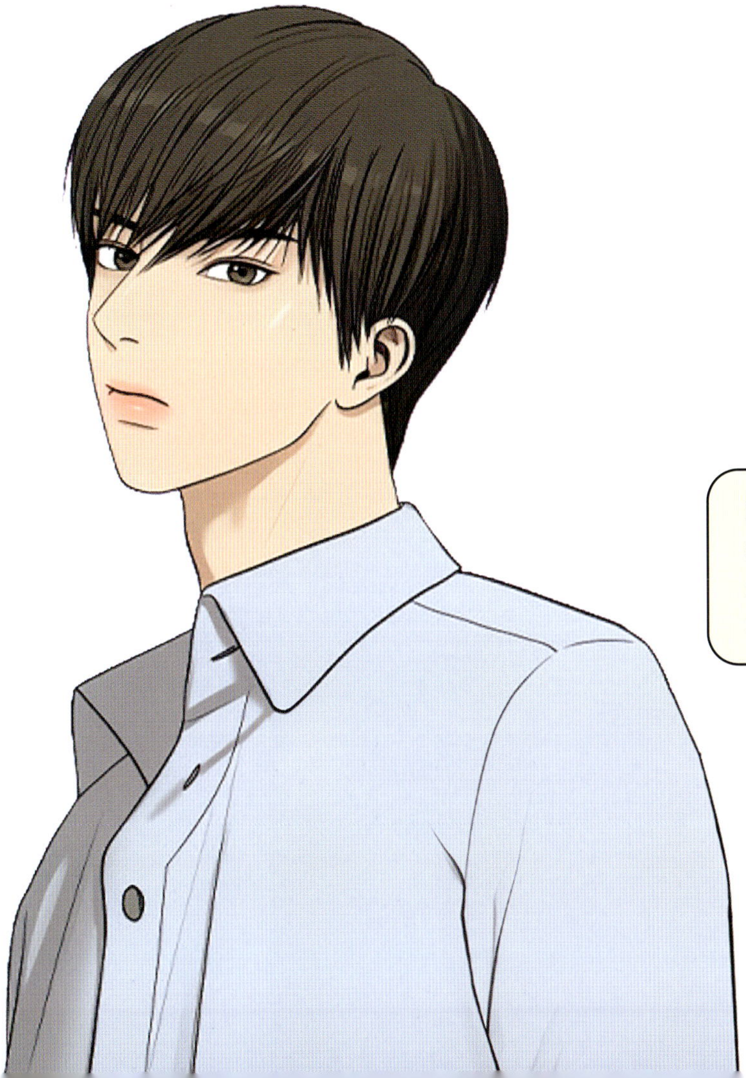

Suho's hair has layered ends that sweep across his forehead. Use a series of parallel lines to give his hair shape and capture his style.

Suho

Body (3/4 View)

Start with a circle for the head. Then add a vertical line to represent the spine. Draw a slanted line to denote the angle of the shoulders. Add broad geometrical shapes for the body, lines for the limbs, and circles for the joints. Continue to fill in the details.

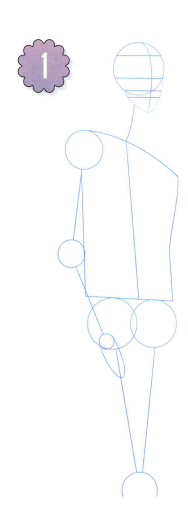

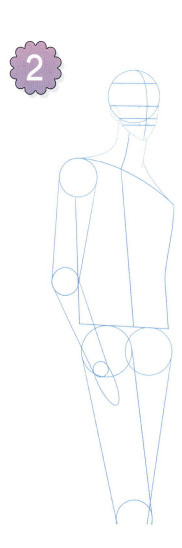

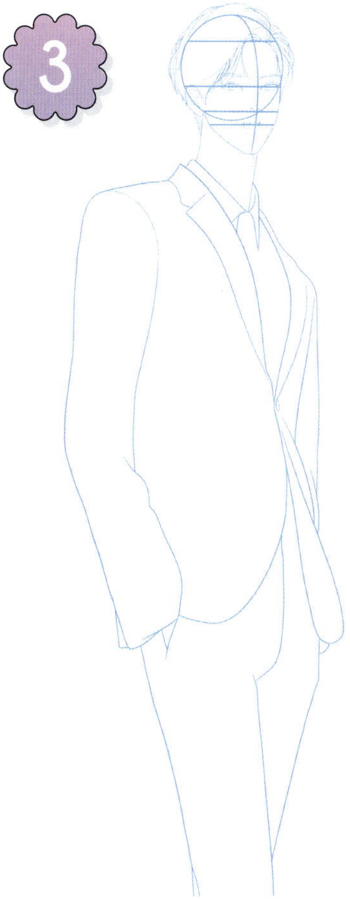
3

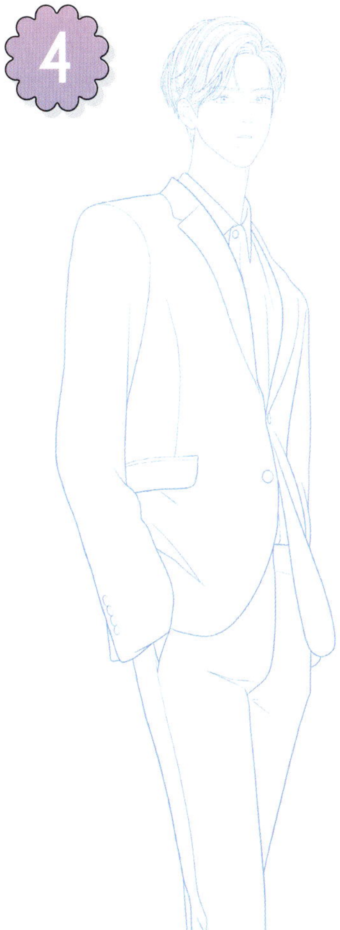
4

Experiment creating this same patterned jacket using a variety of different color combinations. To personalize your art, feel free to change the entire outfit.

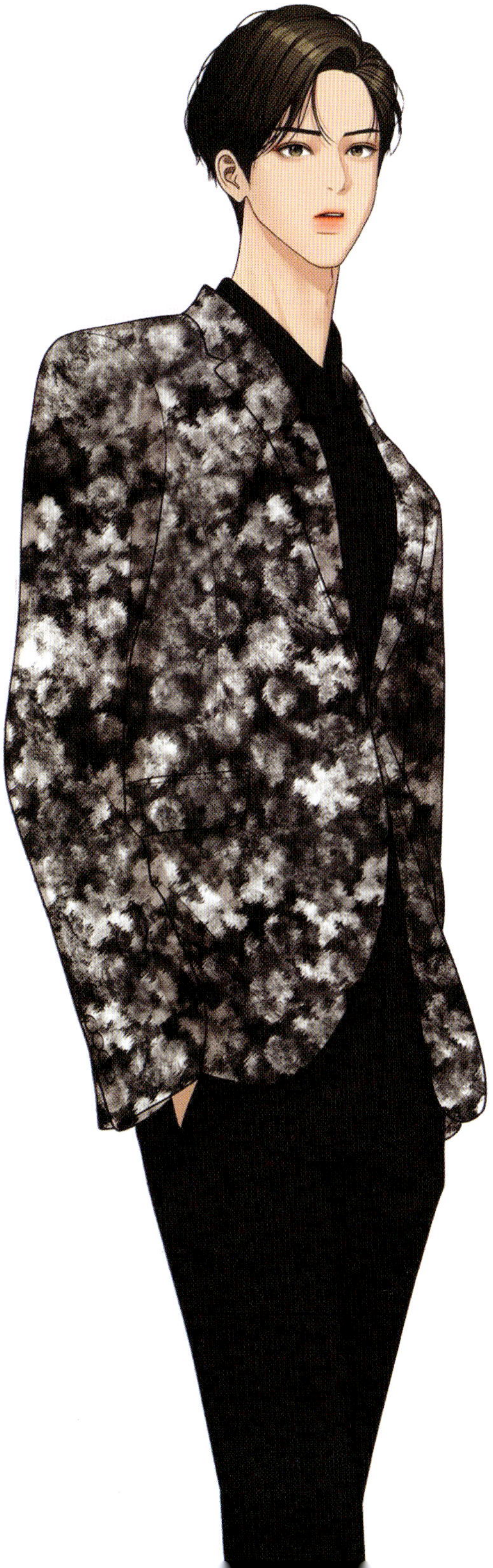

Seo-jun

Head (Front View)

Start with a circle and guidelines to help place the facial features. Next, rough in the shape of the figure. Begin to fill in the details and rough in the eyes, nose, and mouth. Continue to add the details until you are happy with your drawing. Erase old sketch lines and then color your art.

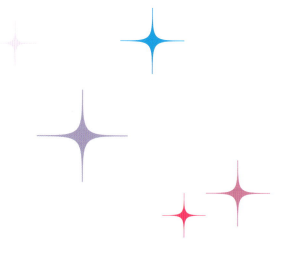

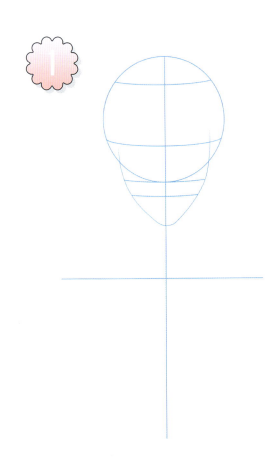

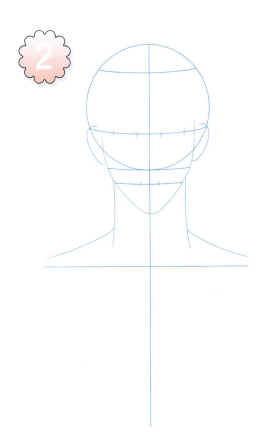

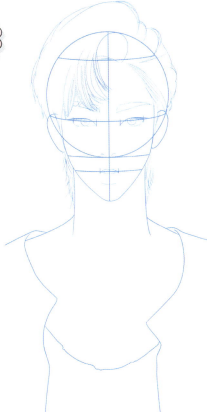

Seo-jun's signature style incorporates a lot of jewelry, including multiple earrings on both ears. When you get to the color stage, add highlights to the chain and earrings to give them a bit of shine.

Seo-jun
Body (Front View)

Start with a circle for the head. Then add a vertical line to represent the spine. Add broad geometrical shapes for the body, lines for the limbs, and circles for the joints. Continue to fill in the details.

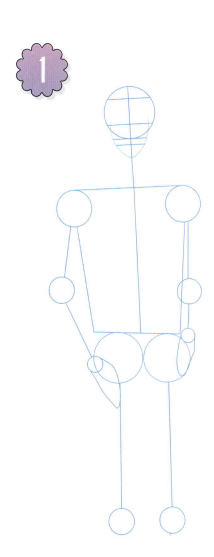

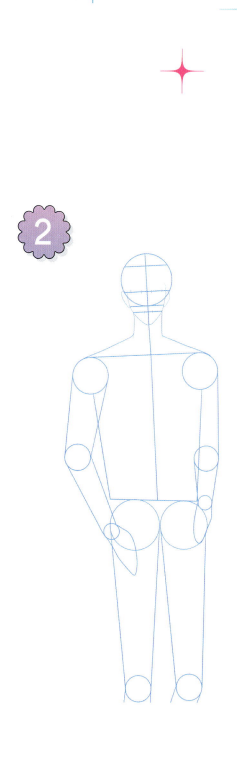

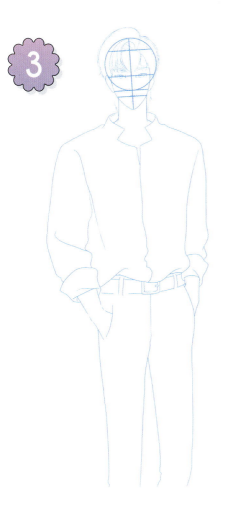

Heavy shading around the right shoulder and down the right arm of Seo-jun's shirt suggests a light source is shining on him at an angle and casting a shadow.

Seo-jun
Head (3/4 View)

Start with a circle for the head. Then add a vertical line to represent the neck and spine. Fill in the shape of the chin so it points at an angle. Add guidelines to the face and draw the features. Continue to follow the steps to complete the drawing.

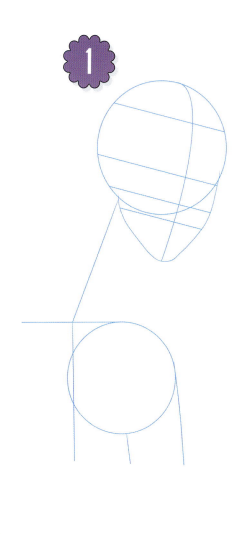

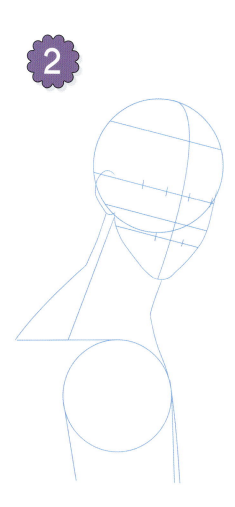

3

Use your color tools to define the muscles in Seo-jun's neck, which is turned at an angle as he looks over his shoulder.

4

Seo-jun
Body (3/4 View)

Start with a circle for the head. Then add a vertical line to represent the spine. Add broad geometrical shapes for the body, lines for the limbs, and circles for the joints. Continue to fill in the details. Erase any old sketch lines and color your drawing.

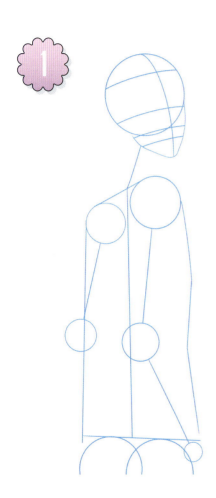

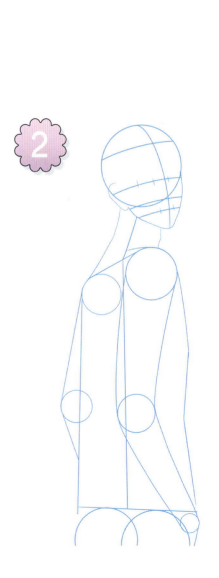

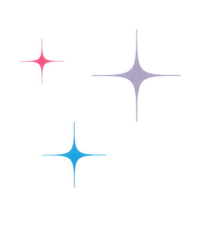

Here, Seo-jun's neck is turned at an angle toward his back. Notice how his chin is in alignment with his shoulder and his wrist.

Suho & Jugyeong

Body (Front View)

Use the same techniques to draw Suho and Jugyeong together as you did when you drew them separately. The only difference is the bit of overlap of their arms. Start by drawing Suho first using a circle for the head and adding guidelines to place the features. Build out his shape and then start drawing Jugyeong. Once you have their basic shapes in place, fill in the details.

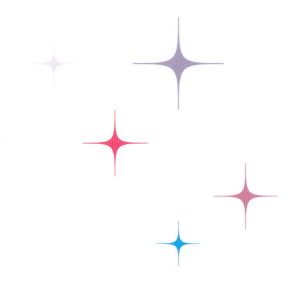

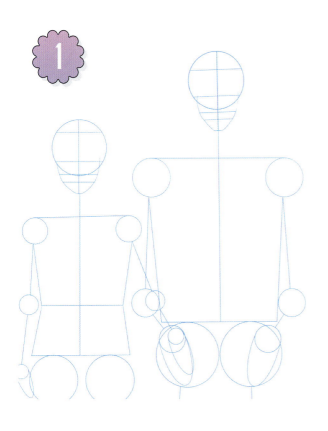

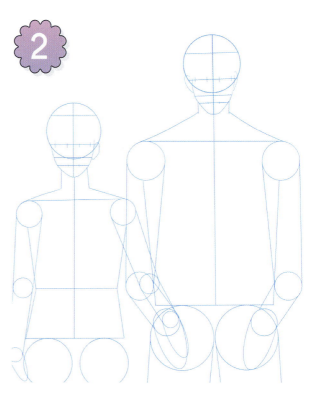

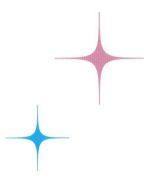

Suho has broad shoulders, whereas Jugyeong is petite by comparison. It helps to draw the biggest figure in a composition first so that you can place smaller figures in relation to the larger figures proportionally.

Seo-jun & Jugyeong

Body (Front View)

Using the same techniques as before, begin by roughing in the head and body frame for both figures. Add their facial features and build out their shapes a little at a time. When you are happy with their shapes, begin adding the details to their clothes and accessories.

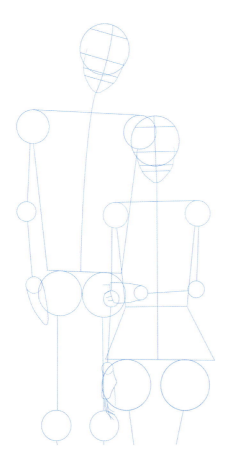

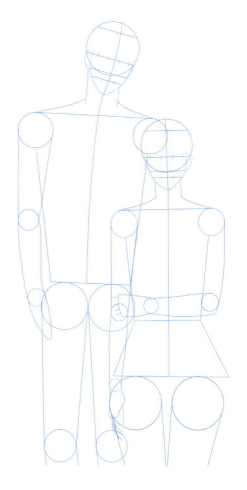

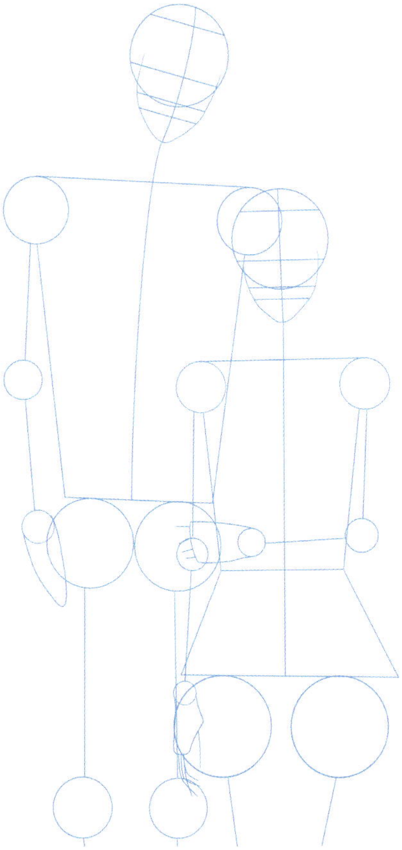

As you grow more comfortable with your drawings, start drawing some basic background elements to place your characters in scenes.

Sua Kang

Head (3/4 View)

Start with a circle and guidelines to help place the facial features. This face is tilted so make sure to adjust your guidelines accordingly. Rough in the shape of the figure and begin to fill in the details. Draw eyes, nose, and mouth. Erase old sketch lines and then add color using the tools of your choice.

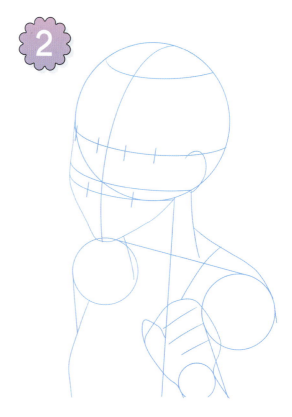

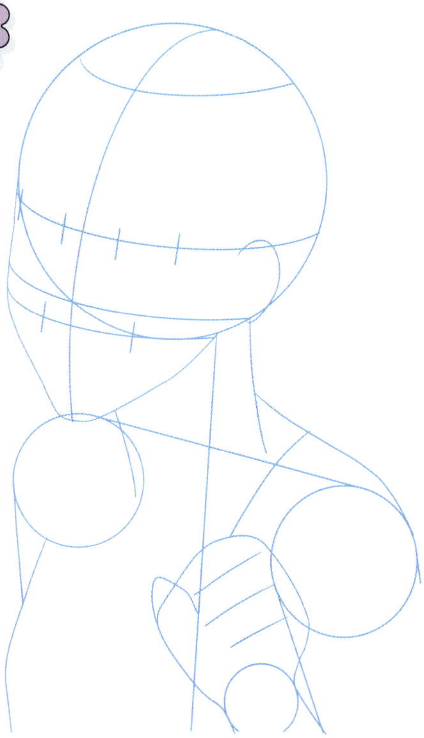

3

Hands are often difficult to draw for beginning artists. Always start with basic lines before attempting to fill in the form. With time and practice, you will be able to render realistic looking hands and fingers.

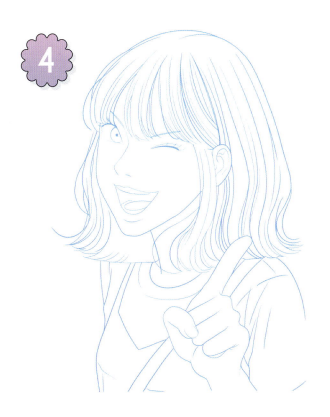

4

69

Sujin Kang

Head (Front View)

Start with a circle for the head. Then add a vertical line to represent the spine. Add broad geometrical shapes for the body, lines for the limbs, and circles for the joints. Continue to fill in the details.

1

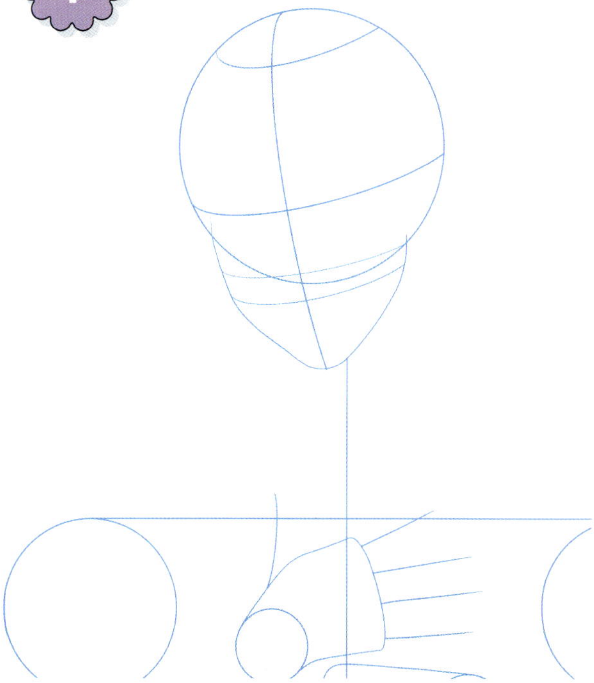

2

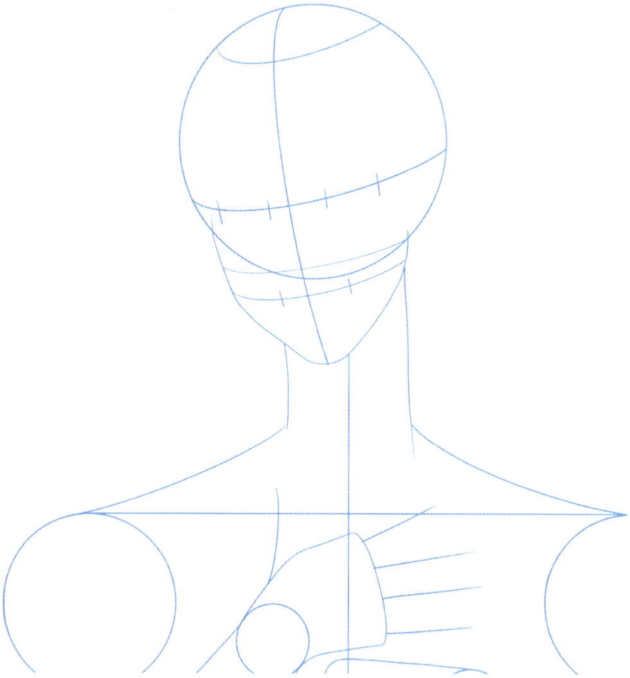

3

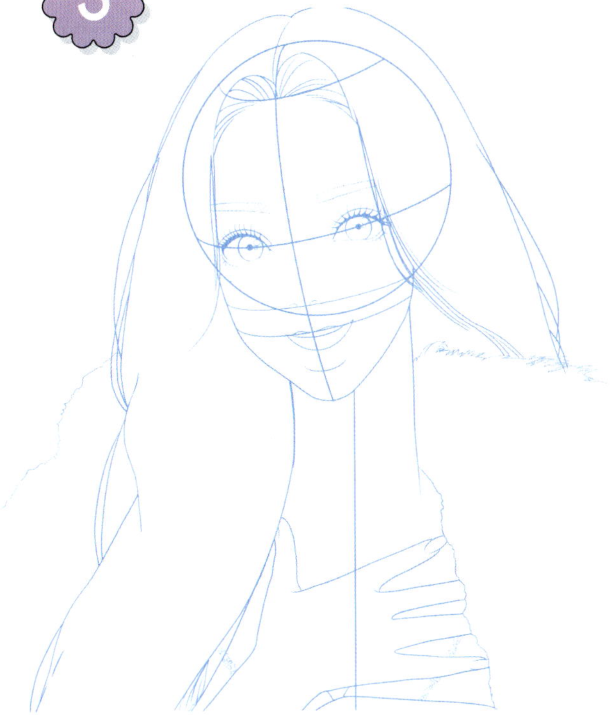

To create a faux fur effect, use a series of hatching and crosshatching strokes to add a textural effect.

4

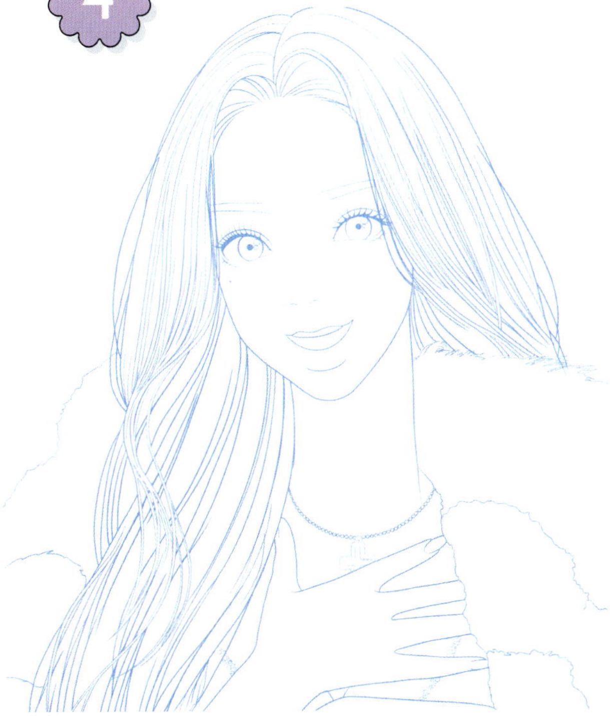

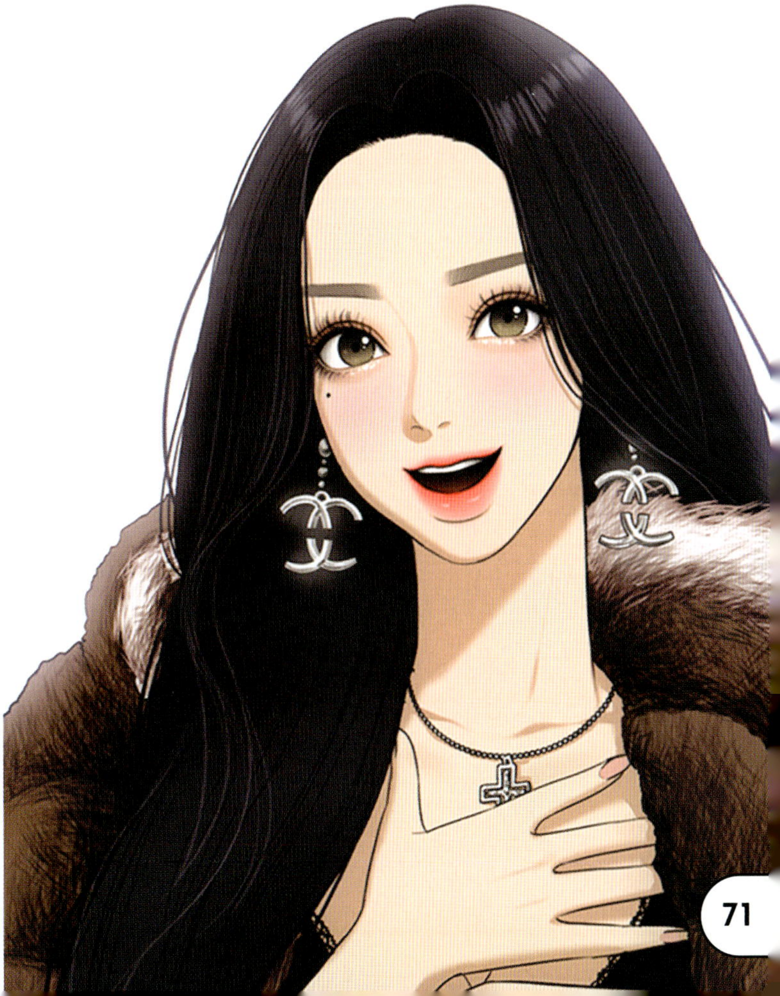

Selena Lee

Head (Front View)

Start with a circle and guidelines to help place the facial features. Next, rough in the shape of the figure. Begin to fill in the details and rough in the eyes, nose, and mouth. Continue to add the details until you are happy with your drawing. Erase old sketch lines and then color your art.

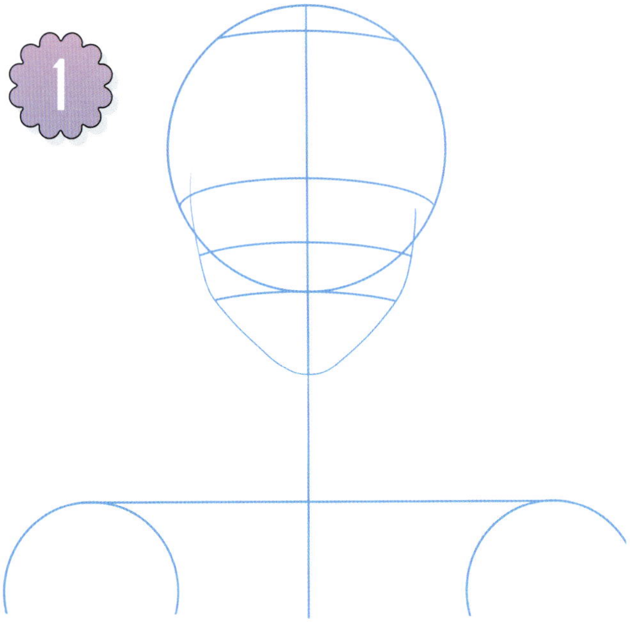
1

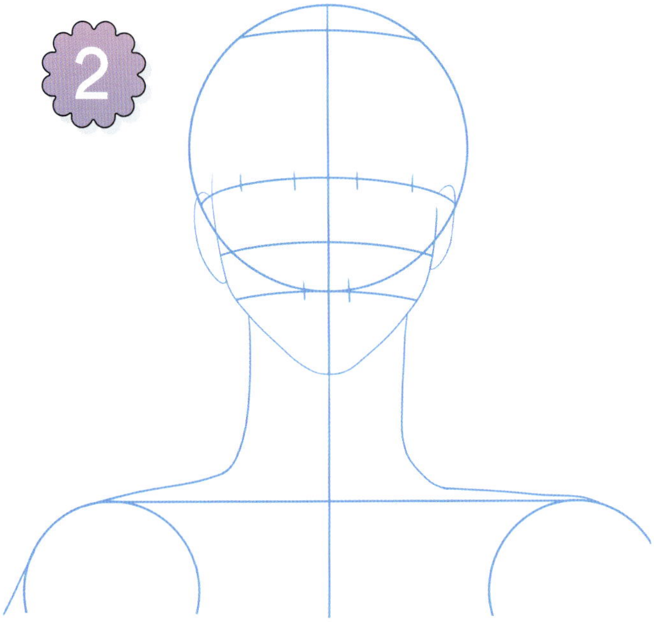
2

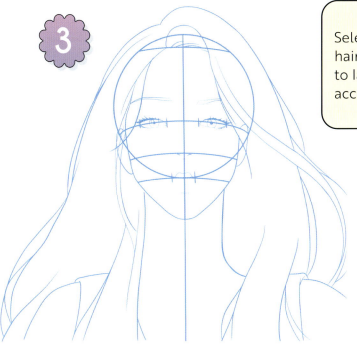

Selena has an ombré color effect in her hair. Use your color and blending tools to layer in subtle color transitions according to your preference.

Makeup

Makeup plays a huge role in True Beauty. In fact, it's almost like another character! Practice drawing lipstick, eye shadow, blush, eye liner, nail polish, and other makeup and beauty tools. Have fun creating color-coordinated makeup palettes for your favorite characters from the series.

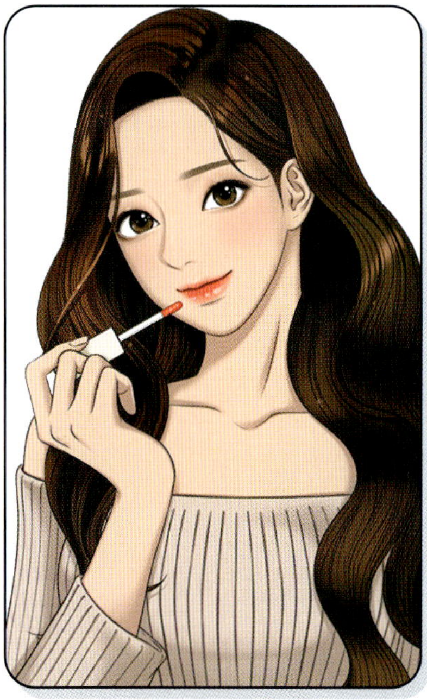

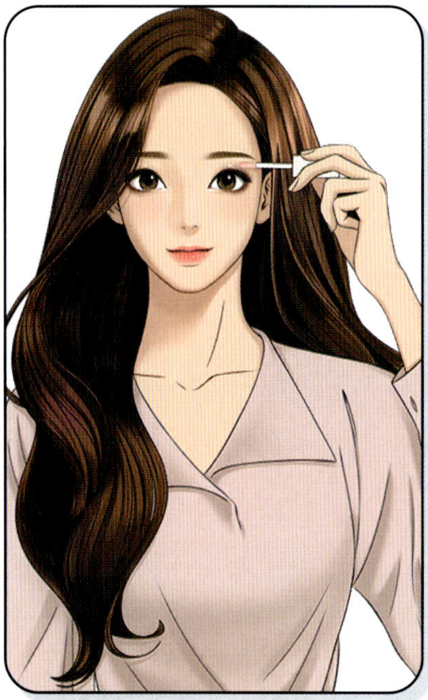

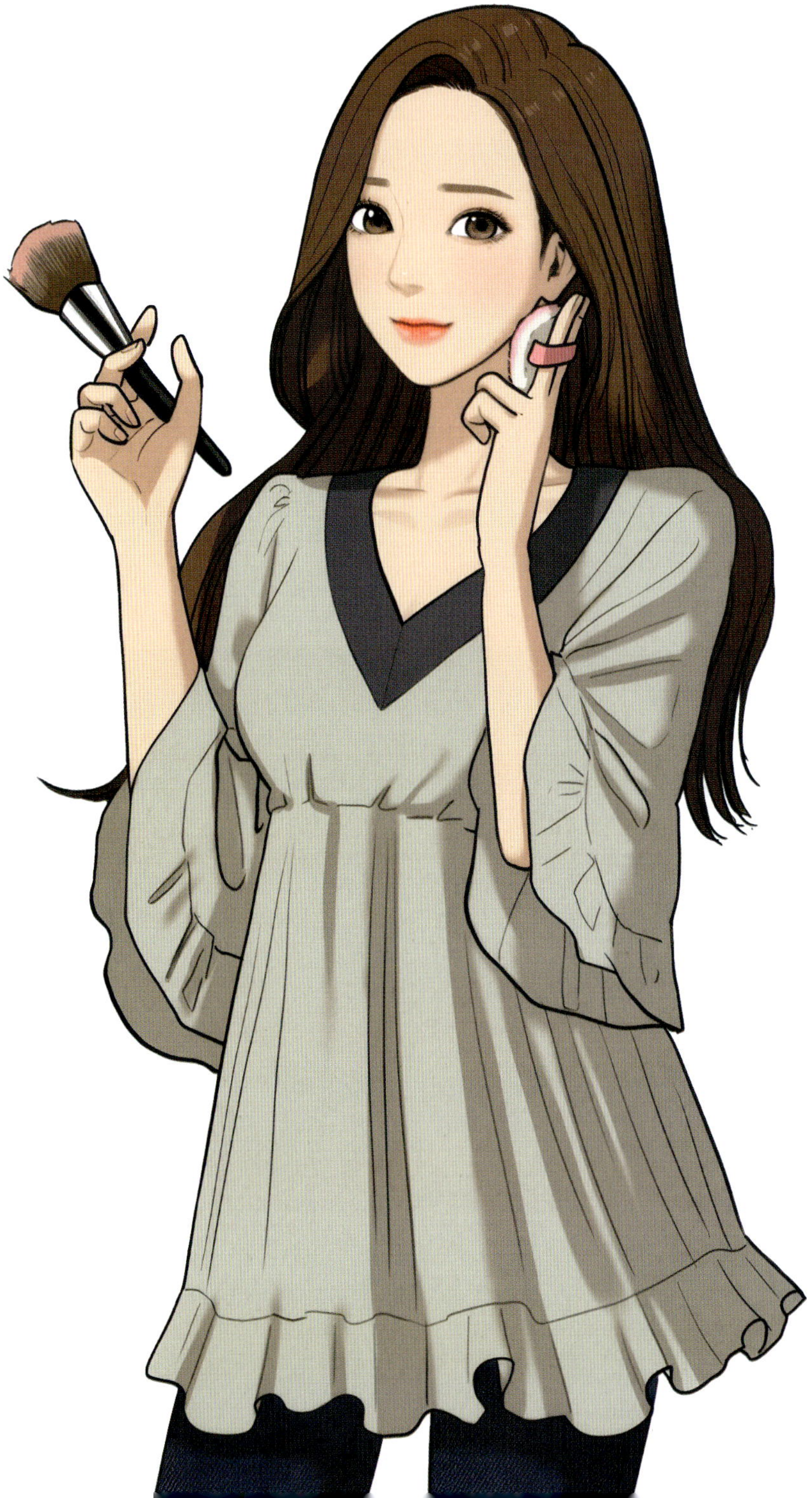

Compact

Eye Shadow Duo

Eye Shadow

Blush

Lipstick

Eye Lash Curler

Contacts

Lighter

BB
CREAM

Cream

Makeup Brush

Nail Polish

Eye Liner

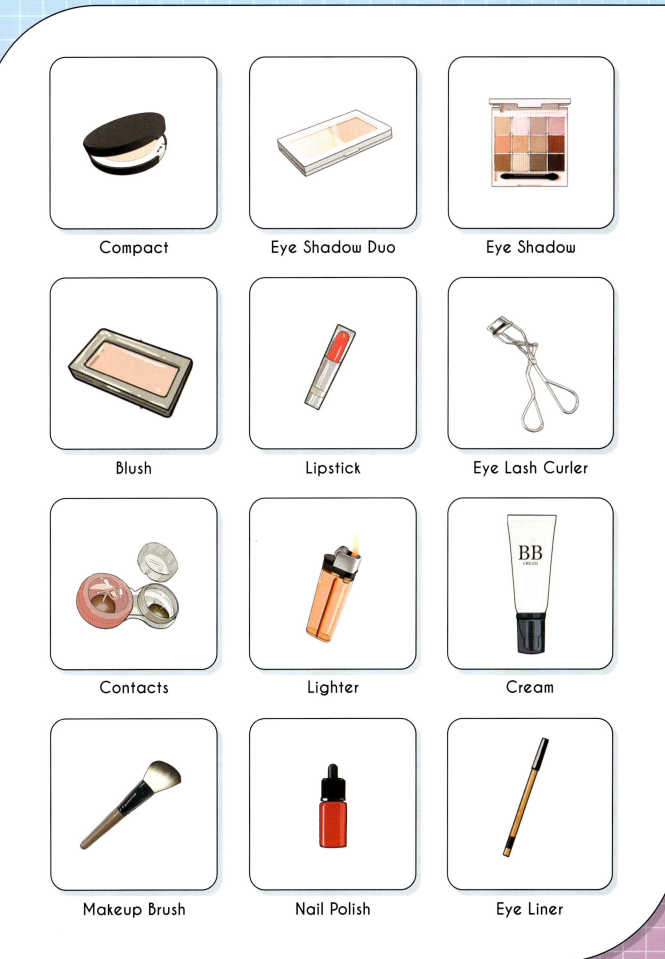

Fashion, Shoes & Accessories

Fashion in True Beauty includes everything from school uniforms, jeans, and T-shirts to high-end designer outfits and couture. And there are plenty of accessories: handbags, fashionable footwear, earrings, bangles, necklaces, and more. Each of the characters has their own distinctive style. As you learn to draw the characters, take some time getting to know their style. Then you can create entirely new wardrobes for them.

Jugyeong's Style

Jugyeong's style changes throughout the series and gets gradually more sophisticated. She rotates outfits that include a school uniform, sporty clothes, casual outfits, and designer fashions.

Straight hair

Zip-up hoodie

Pleated uniform skirt

Knee-high socks

Sneakers

Backpack

High ponytail
Loose hair strand
Sporty T-shirt and drawstring shorts combo
Sliders

False eyelashes
Sparkly barrettes
Statement earrings
Brooch

High heels

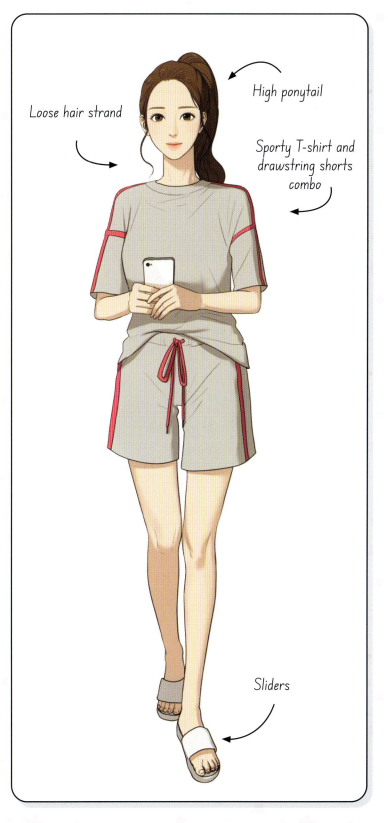

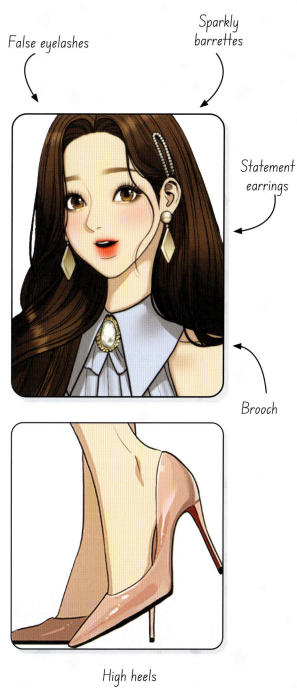

Developing a Character's Style

When designing character clothing, think about their needs as people moving through the story universe. Where are they going? Who are they meeting? What activities will they be participating in? Use details from your storytelling to inform the clothes they wear.

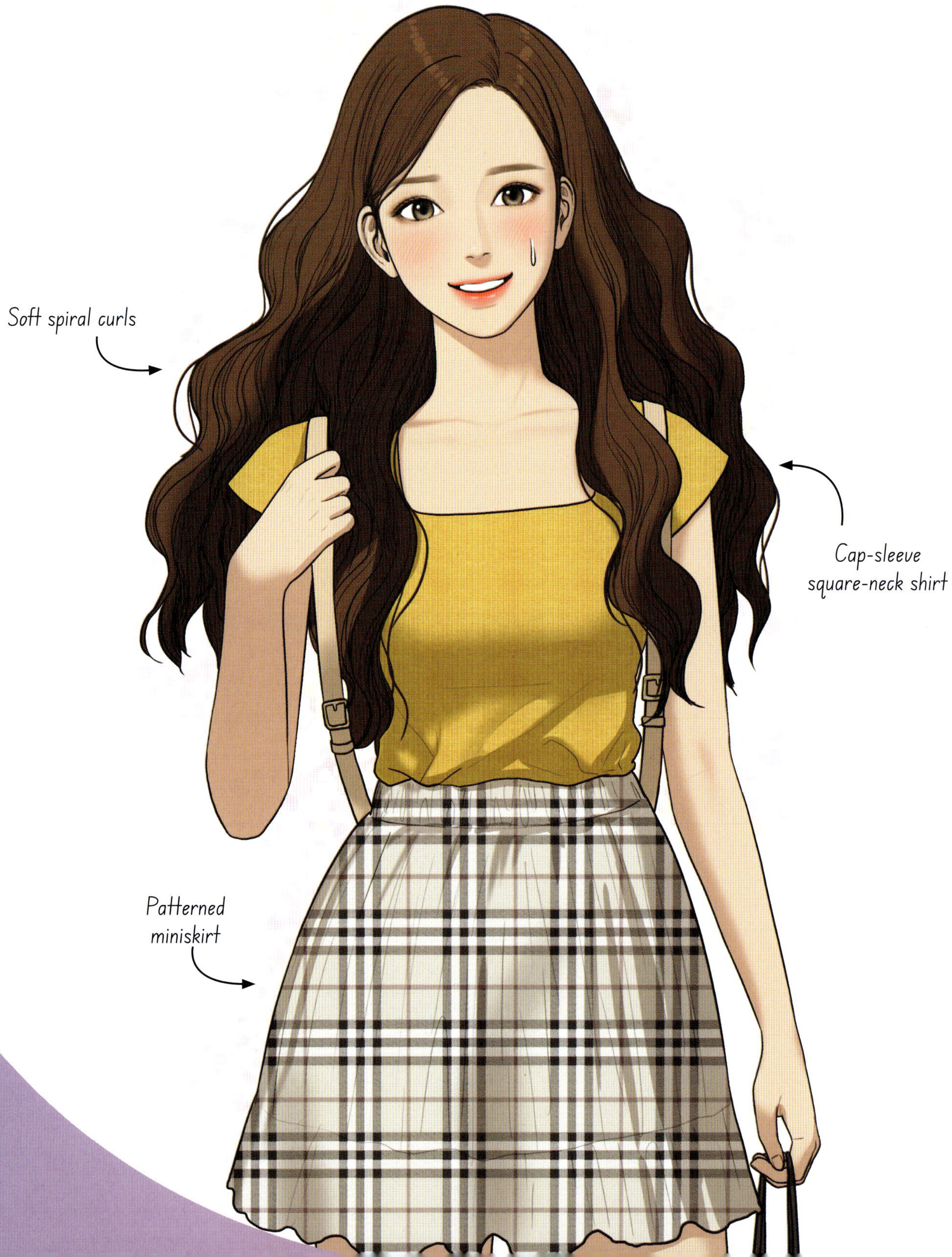

Soft spiral curls
Cap-sleeve square-neck shirt
Patterned miniskirt

Special Occasions

Imagine your characters in various scenes and in different places, such as on vacation, at fancy dinners, and attending formal events like weddings. Design a line of fashions to match each character's style and personality to the outfit for the occasion. Once you've designed the clothes, design the accessories, including shoes and jewelry. Finally, create hairstyles and makeup palettes.

- V-neck ruffle blouse
- Wavy hair
- Bracelet
- Ruffle miniskirt
- Designer handbag
- Open-toed heels

Experiment with mixing and matching Jugyeong's outfits and accessories from across the series to give her new looks that are personalized to your own art style.

Suho's Style

Suho's style is trendy yet understated. He enjoys wearing sophisticated designer clothes in addition to casual everyday jeans and T-shirts. His look is more conservative than Seo-jun's style, but it suits his personality well.

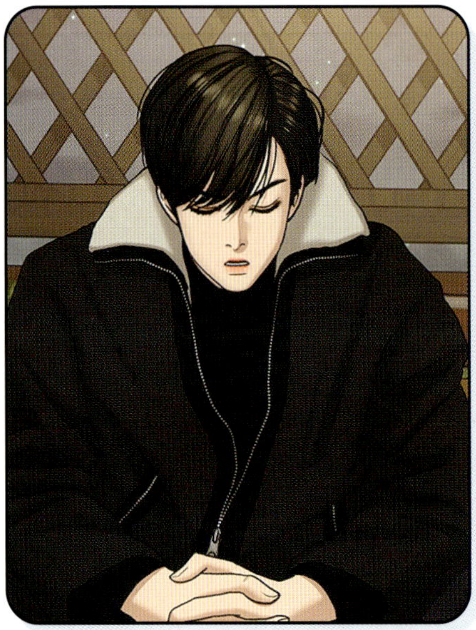

Bomber jacket

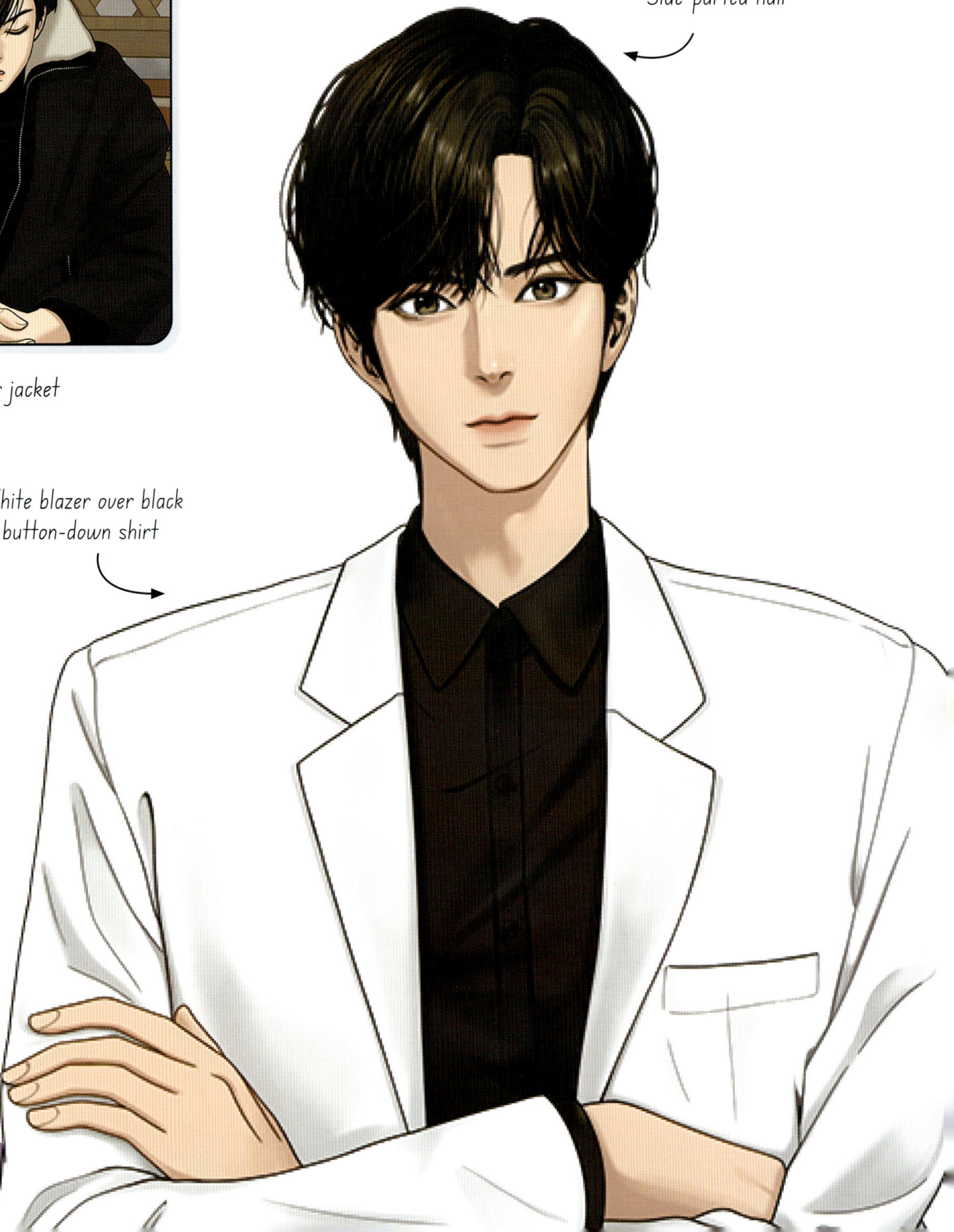
Side-parted hair
White blazer over black button-down shirt

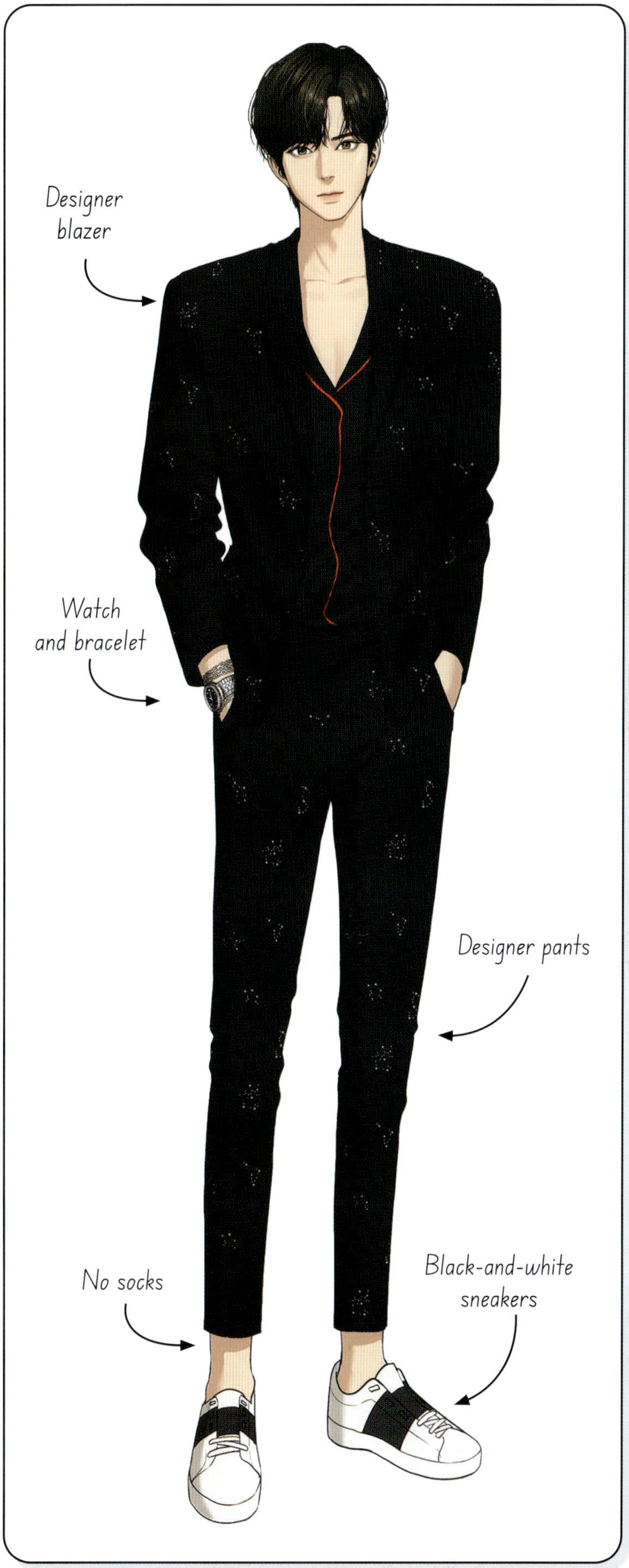
Designer
blazer
Watch
and bracelet
Designer pants
No socks
Black-and-white
sneakers

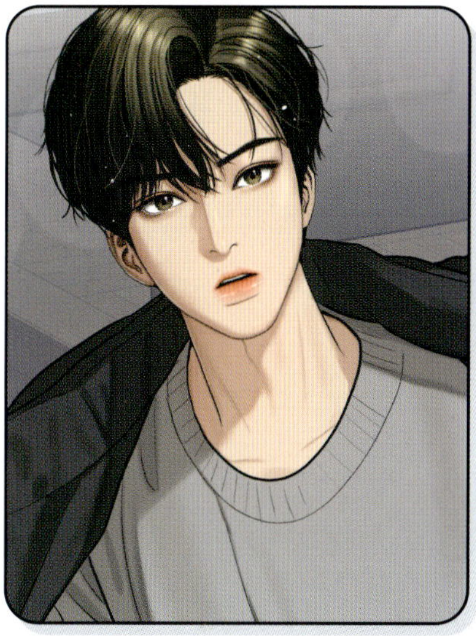

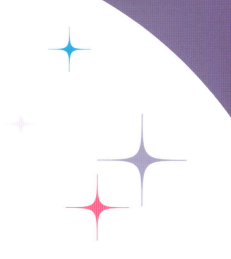

Jacket over sweater

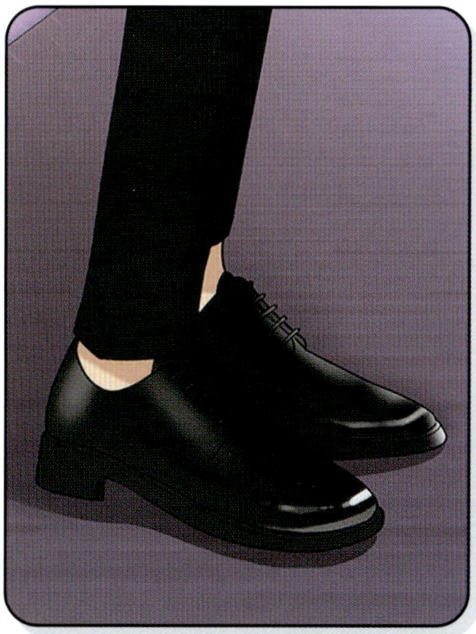

Black dress shoes

Seo-jun's Style

Seo-jun embraces an edge to his style, and he likes to mix things up so his look is personal to him. He loves patterned shirts and ripped jeans, and you'll rarely see him without his signature bracelets, ear cuff, and earrings. He likes to wear a pocket chain as well as hats.

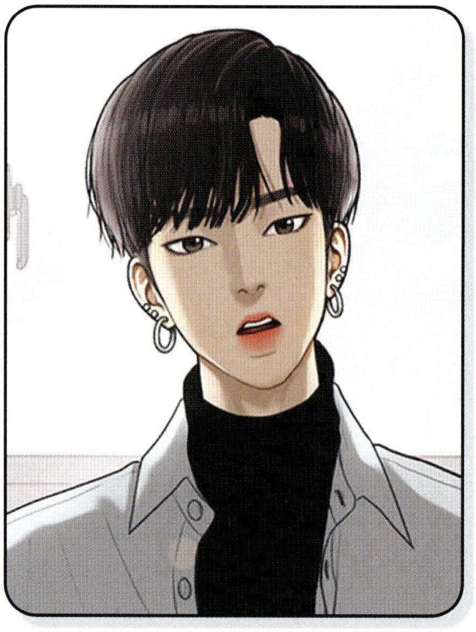

Seo-jun often wears a combination of hoop and stud earrings on both ears.

Wispy hair strands sweep forehead.

Trendy patterned shirt

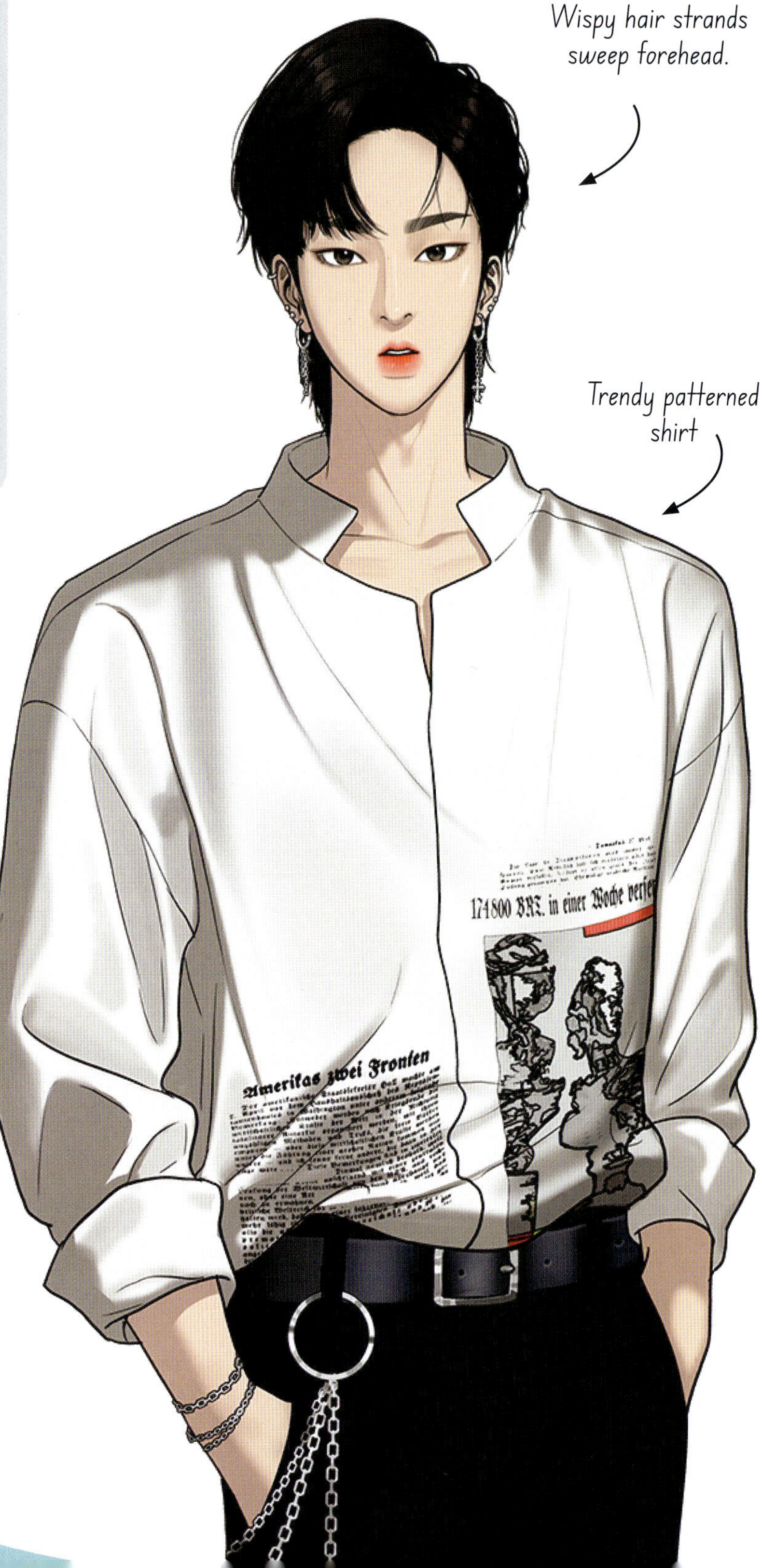
Amerikas zwei Fronten

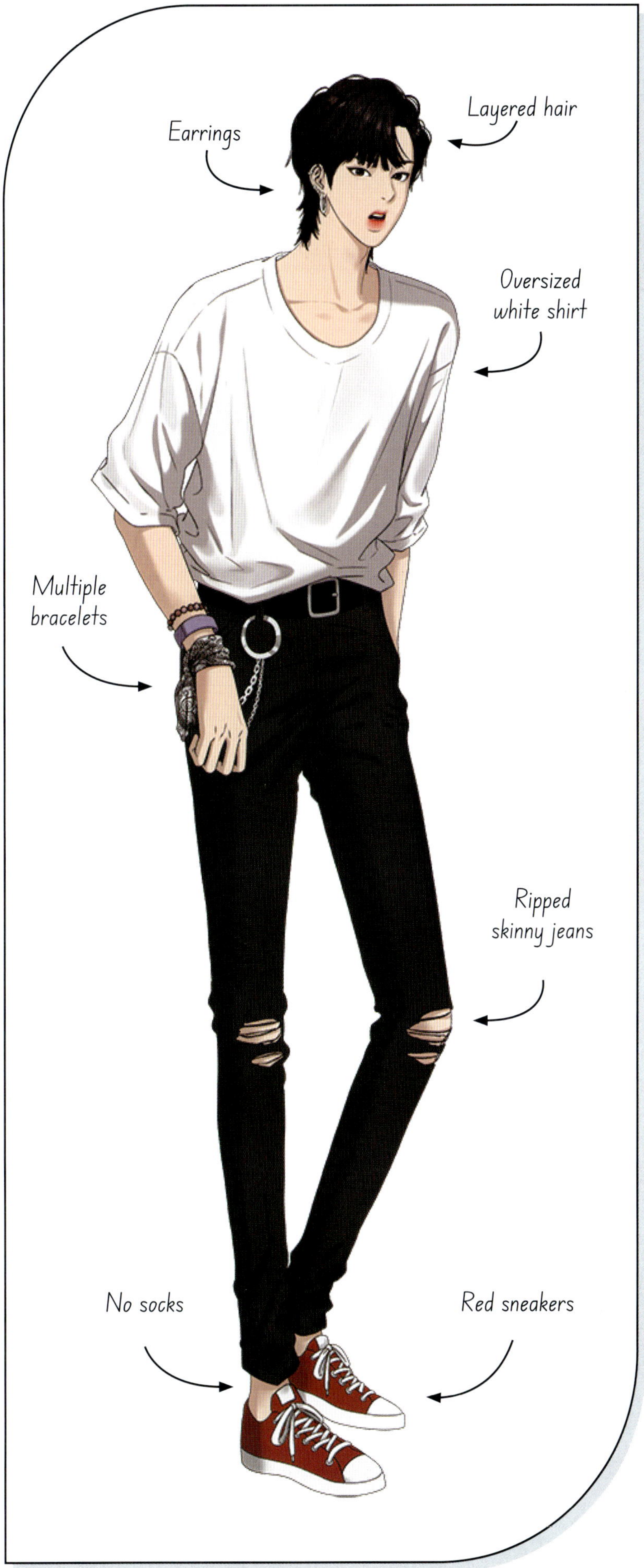
Earrings
Layered hair
Oversized white shirt
Multiple bracelets
Ripped skinny jeans
No socks
Red sneakers

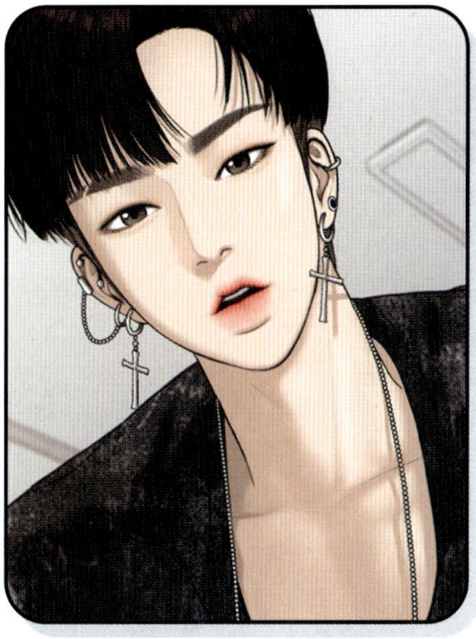

Cross earrings

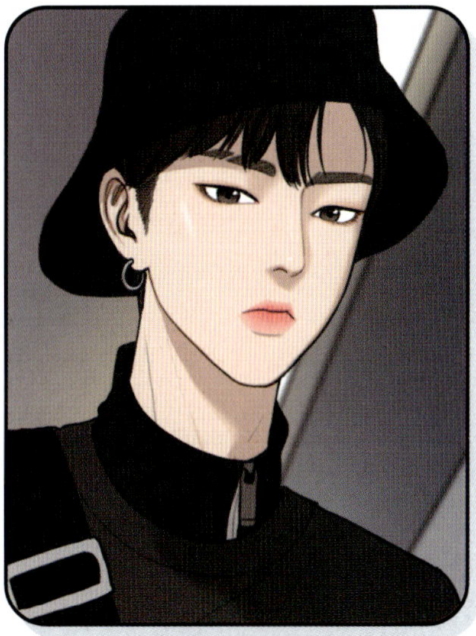

Bucket hat

Mastering Details

Details can make or break a piece of artwork. In True Beauty, the characters are meticulous about their makeup, hair, and clothes, so it's important to pay attention to small, seemingly insignificant things, such as the clasps on a handbag or the stitching of a sweater. Clothes should look natural to the character's form and figure.

Every garment a character wears is affected by the force of gravity pulling on it, how heavy the fabric is, and how much it stretches or drapes on the body.

Jacket drapes casually over the shoulder.

Darker shading on the tank top shows the natural shadow cast by the jacket.

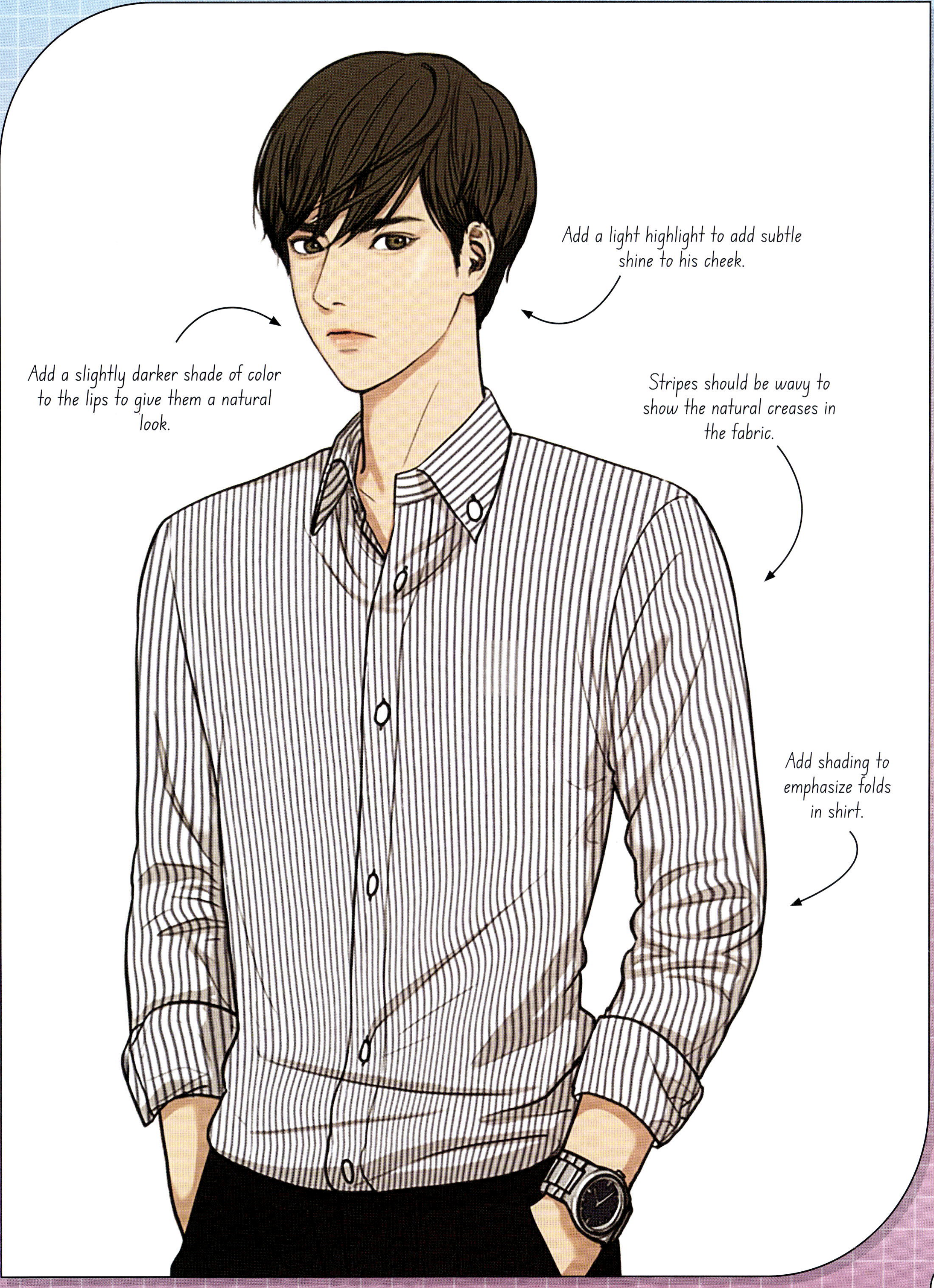
Add a light highlight to add subtle shine to his cheek.
Add a slightly darker shade of color to the lips to give them a natural look.
Stripes should be wavy to show the natural creases in the fabric.
Add shading to emphasize folds in shirt.

ANALOGOUS: THREE COLORS NEXT TO EACH OTHER

COMPLEMENTARY: OPPOSITES ON THE COLOR WHEEL

Adding Color

A color wheel can be divided into categories: primary, secondary, tertiary, complementary, and analogous colors. Red, yellow, and blue are primary colors, and the rest are derived from various mixtures of these primaries. A complementary color offers the most contrast to its matching primary color.

When illustrating scenes, it's helpful to think about the intensity and variety of color, which means tone, saturation, and contrast. For a series like True Beauty, it's extra fun to assign colors to certain characters in order to highlight their fashion tastes and sensibilities. Look through your favorite scenes and try to notice how the use of color draws your eye from panel to panel.

When creating your own art, reference the color wheel to help you plan the palette that will bring your stories to life!

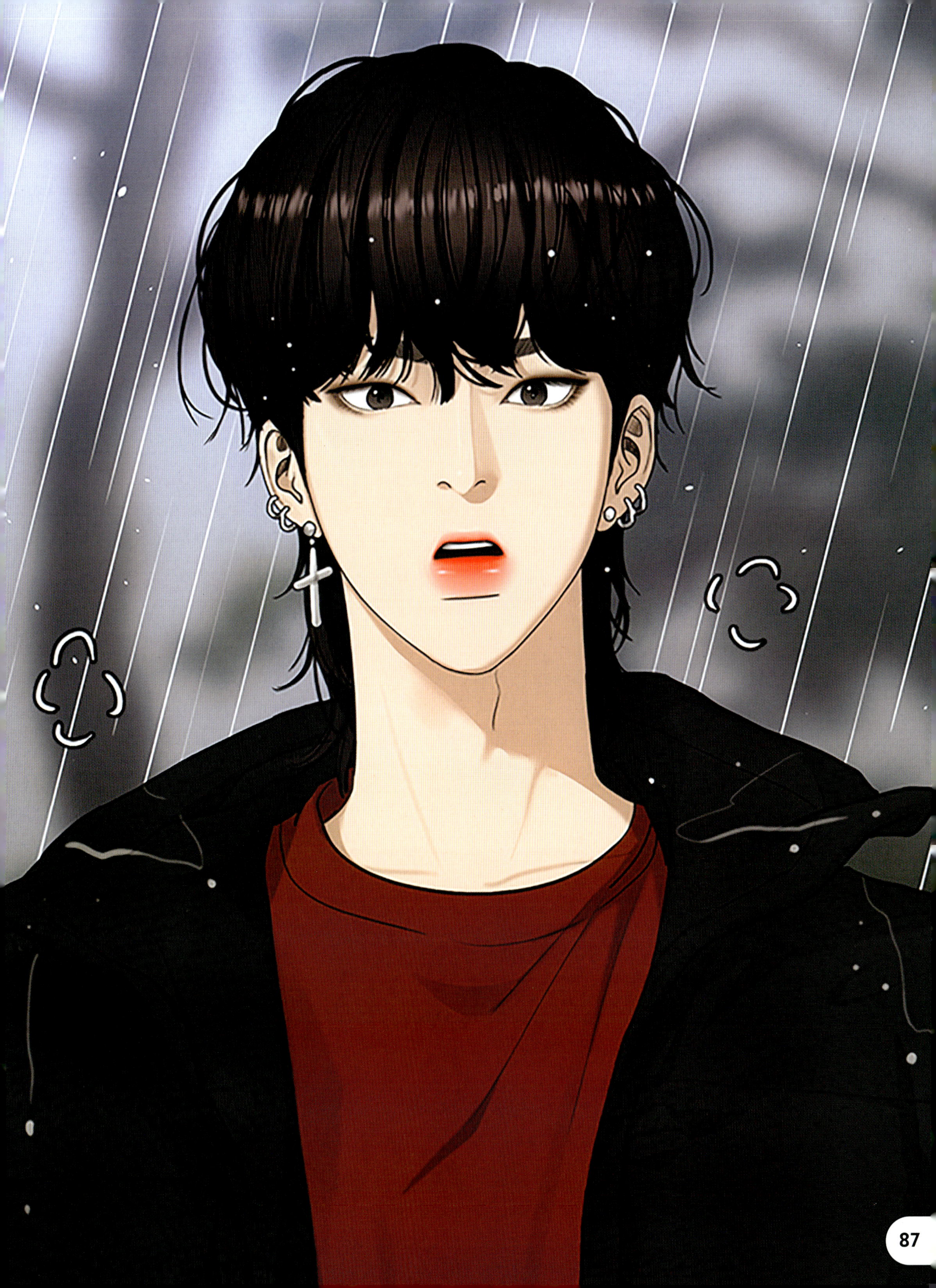

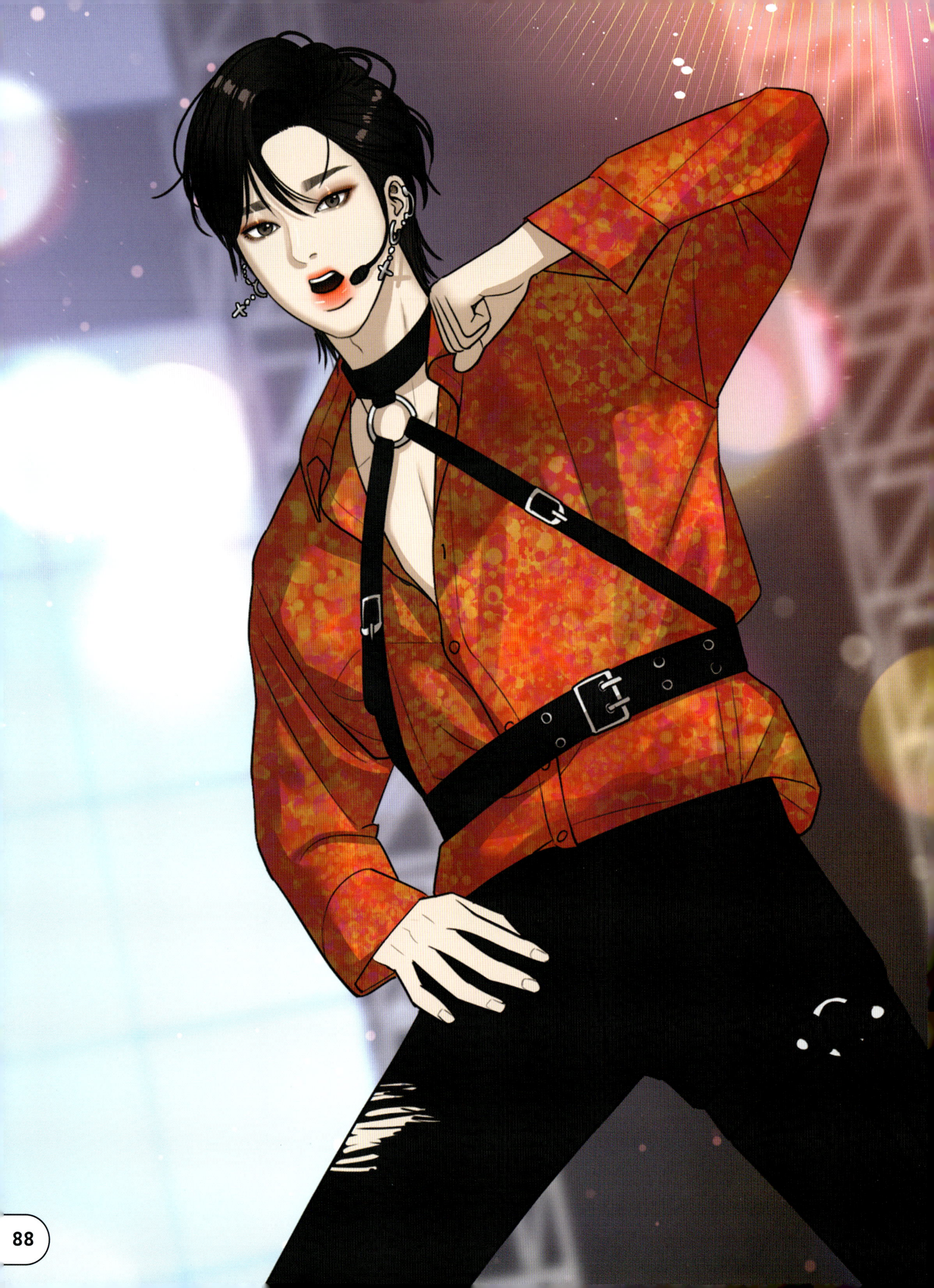

Creating Atmosphere with Light

When placing your characters in various scenes and settings, how the image is lit can play a huge role in setting the atmosphere, mood, and tone of the scene. Try to keep the light sources consistent within your scenes and always consider the time of day.

Light is also a wonderful tool for drawing the reader's eye, adding visual interest and texture to backgrounds and settings, and making scenes feel dynamic and authentic.

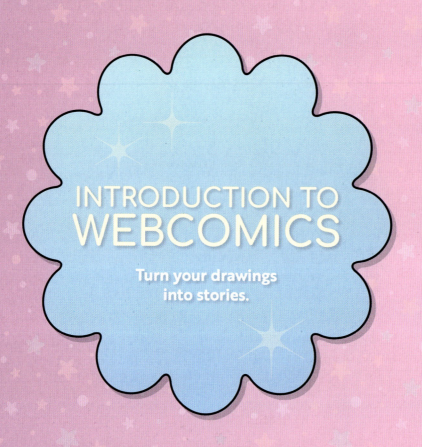

INTRODUCTION TO WEBCOMICS

Turn your drawings into stories.

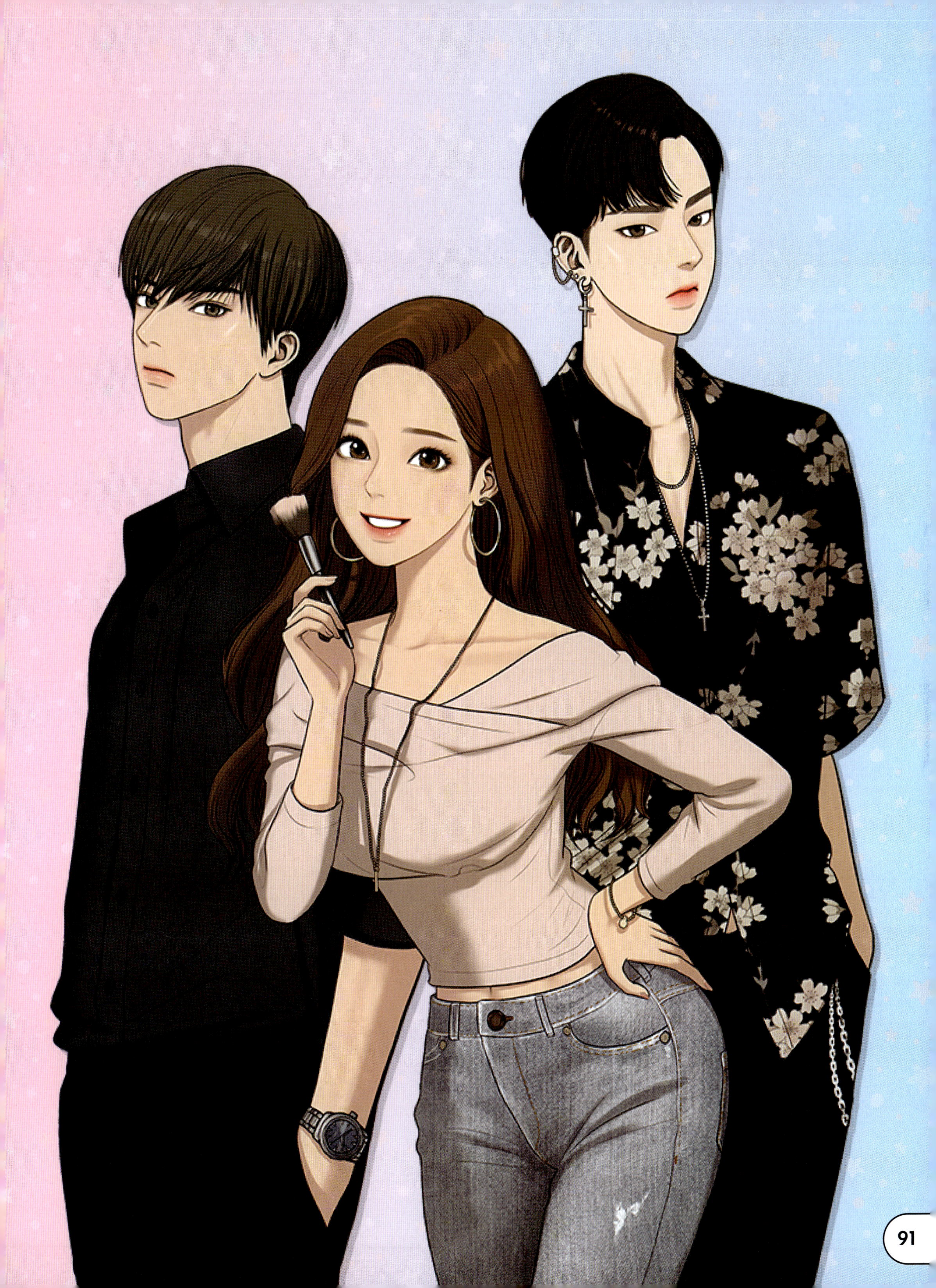

Introduction to Publishing on WEBTOON

WEBTOON introduced a new way to create stories for anyone who has a story to tell. If you want to publish your own webcomic, your story can start with CANVAS, WEBTOON's self-publishing platform.

Posting on CANVAS means that you, as a creator, have control over all aspects of your story and can use the platform to build a unique audience thanks to the thousands of readers that visit the platform daily.

Some of WEBTOON's most popular titles began on WEBTOON CANVAS. WEBTOON Originals are stories that are developed for the platform.

Unlike traditional comics, which are meant to be read in a print format, WEBTOON is a mobile-based platform, so the content has been formatted to be read vertically.

Through the vertical format, reading a WEBTOON series is meant to feel like a cinematic experience since the reader can see only one panel at a time instead of the entire page like in a traditional print comic.

If you have a story to tell and want to create your own webcomic, it takes planning.

DEVELOP YOUR CHARACTERS

Creating believable characters is one of the most important tasks for any creator. When developing a character for your story, consider these parameters in order to have a good understanding of who they are; this will ground the character in your story and make them seem more believable to the reader:

- What is their role in the story?
- What is this character's intended arc? A character arc is usually the internal journey a character goes through over the course of the story.
- What are their strengths and weaknesses?
- What relationships do they have with other characters in the story?
- What is their motivation?

CREATE CHARACTER SHEETS

- Character Designs / Physical
- Characteristics / Color Palette
- Motivations (Wants vs. Needs)
- Mannerisms, Perks, and Flaws
- Circle of Being (Backstory)

PLAN YOUR STORY

What is the setting?

This is the location of the action that includes time and place (when and where).

What is the overall plot of your story?

The plot is the actual story. A plot should have a beginning, middle, and end, with a clear conflict and resolution:

- Conflict is usually a problem the plot is intended to resolve; without conflict, there's no story to tell.
- Resolution is the solution to the main conflict of the story. It's important to make sure the resolution feels earned by wrapping up the main story conflict, character arcs, and setting.

CREATE YOUR COMIC

THUMBNAILS

This is when you plan out your panels based on your story. Thumbnails are intended to be very loose, simple drawings that will help you to have an understanding of how the episode will be structured. Storyboarding an episode can help creators plan scenes and sequences with pacing, clarity, and readability in mind for readers.

SKETCHES

Once you've created your rough thumbnails, you're ready to start sketching your characters and backgrounds. This is also the stage when creators plan out the placement of their speech bubbles.

INKING

Inking is the process of cleaning up your lines to create a more polished look.

COLORING & FINALIZING

Add color, speech bubbles, special effects, and lettering.

Storytelling in Drawing

When drawing webcomics, you need to pack a lot of action and storytelling into a small frame and with limited dialogue, so every detail counts. This is where backgrounds, character poses, and expressions all come together to form a complete picture. Once these crucial elements are in place, you can add impactful dialogue to move the storyline forward.

Start with a thumbnail to establish your scenes and storyboards. Then, sketch your scene. This is where you'll refine the piece and add all of the subtle details that add depth to the storytelling. Erase any old sketch marks and ink your drawing.

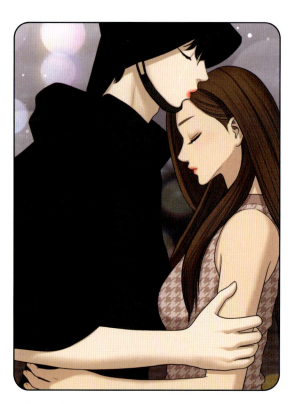

The color stage is where you get to enhance the mood of your scene. Use soft muted tones to underscore tender moments between the characters.

Each of these scenes tells a story without using dialogue. In addition to facial expressions, body language can help reveal a character's mindset, motivation, or internal conflict. Paying extra attention to these details can help set the tone of your story, while adding to its believability. Take a look at the sketches and final color art below. How do the actions of the characters reveal the story?

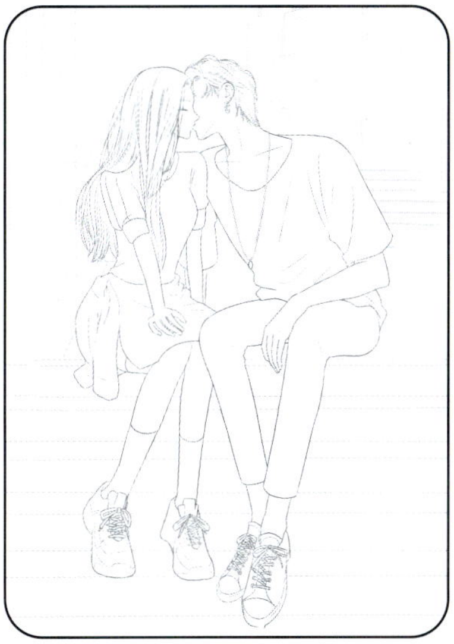
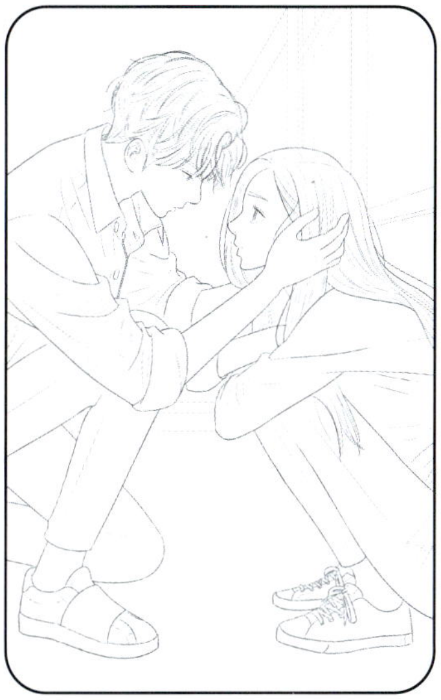
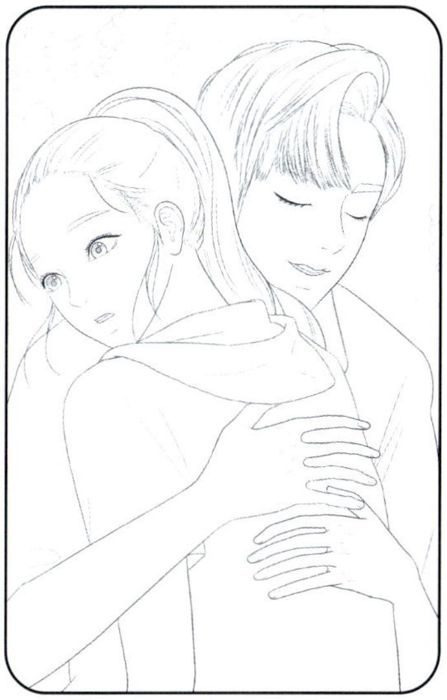

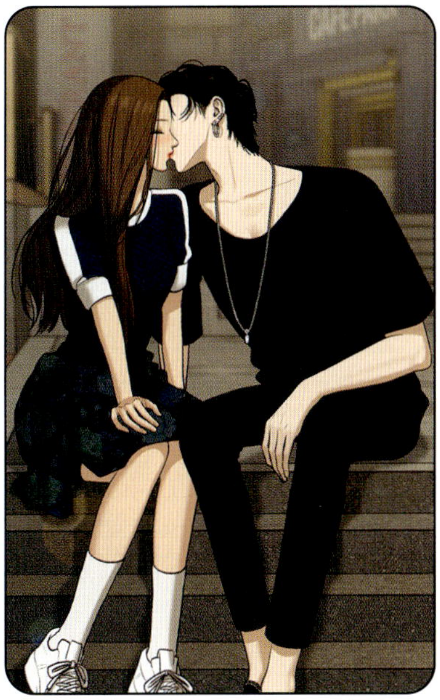
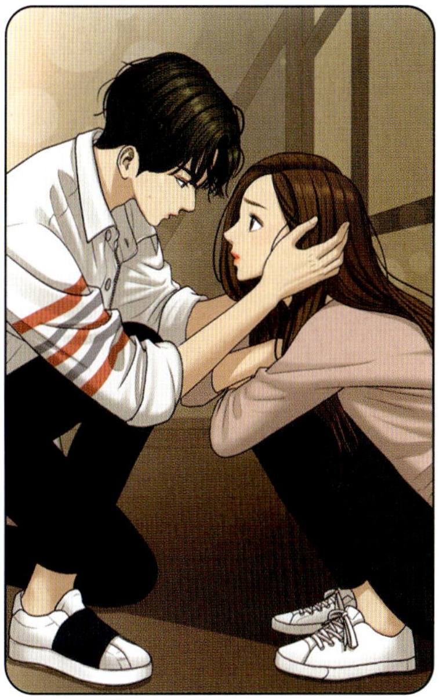
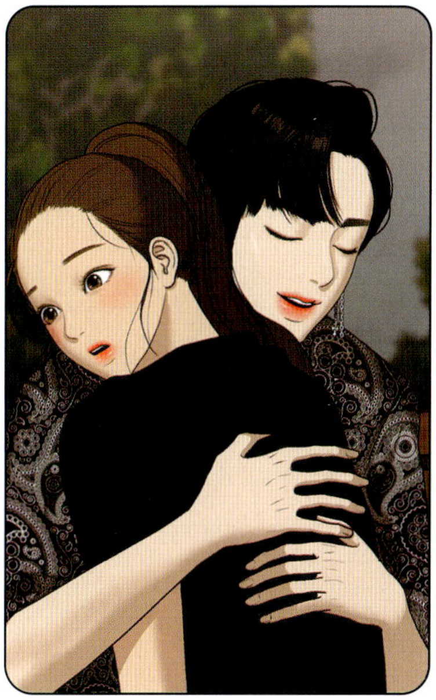

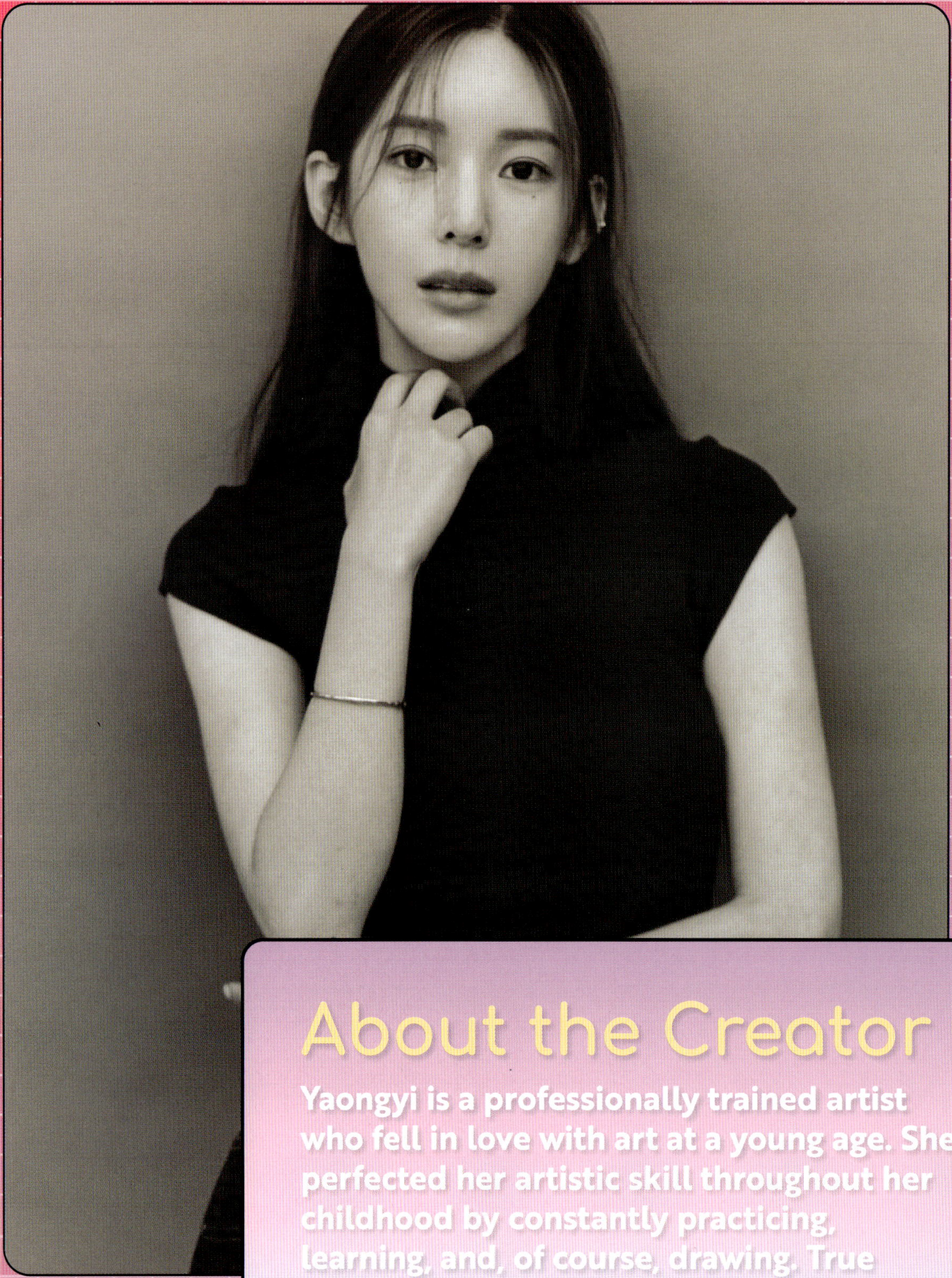

About the Creator

Yaongyi is a professionally trained artist who fell in love with art at a young age. She perfected her artistic skill throughout her childhood by constantly practicing, learning, and, of course, drawing. True Beauty is her first webcomic, and she's thrilled to share her characters with readers in this new illustrative way.

For more from Yaongyi, check out:
Instagram: @meow91_